THE LAND OF
PROMISE

BILLY KRIEG

authorHOUSE®

AuthorHouse™
1663 Liberty Drive
Bloomington, IN 47403
www.authorhouse.com
Phone: 1-800-839-8640

First published by AuthorHouse 4/04/2011

ISBN: 978-1-4567-3684-2 (e)
ISBN: 978-1-4567-3683-5 (sc)

Library of Congress Control Number: 2011902704

Printed in the United States of America

TABLE OF CONTENTS

PREFACE

THE PURPOSE OF LEARNING HISTORY is to learn about the nature of man by studying his past which should make it possible to predict to some extent what men will do in the future.

Most people learn their history from their high school or college textbooks that teachers teach from which tells about kings, emperors, dictators, presidents corrupt politicians and what these people say they did and how heroic they said they were. These people are exceptions and it is difficult to tell the nature of man by studying the exceptions, especially when these exceptions give us prejudicial information.

But the average person that makes up 99.999 per cent of the population goes unnoticed by historians. How accurate can history be if it ignores the people it is supposed to be about? But those who write history would rather get information from the few exception rather than trying to get information from millions of ordinary people who do not have keep records.

But these ordinary families often have information that is handed down in families and interesting stories are often recorded for the descendents.

The Promised Land is a story of two waifs, a male and a female in London who are shipped to a prison in the American Colonies for a very minor offense. Upon release, they find themselves in the colonies. This is the story of about how the Carters survived and created an American dynasty. This book covers two generations of the Carter family. The history of the first generation was recorded by an attorney as dictated by the first Carter to immigrate to America. The second half of the book was recorded by Carter's daughter-in-law.

This is the story of how two generations of Carters beginning in 1763 and ending in 1843 experienced war, financial panic, epidemics crooked politicians, ineffective government and environmental disasters that happened during this period.

Learning how they survived these tragedies will help the reader better understand American History.

1763-1843

MY NAME IS EZRA HAZARD, Mr. Crinan Carter's Solicitor in Memphis Town. Since he cannot read or write, he has asked me to write down what he tells me. He wants it written down so that his descendents will see that ideas and hard work will not only make people successful but will make them happy. He begins his story by explaining how he and Mary, his wife, met.

CHAPTER I
WHEN WE MET

I WAS ON THE ROAD TO LONDON when I looked through the bushes along the road and saw a turnip patch. I remember thinking that the bloody fog would hide me when I pulled them up and was surprised when I heard someone say, "Would you pull some for me too? I'm so hungry I'm weak." Well, there was nothing else I could do but pull up a few more for whoever was on the road.

Had to get up right close in the fog to see that the voice was that of a very small girl. She was a pretty one too. Said her name was Mary O'Kane.

"Where you going?" I asked.

"I don't know."

"Where did you come from?"

"I don't know."

While I was trying to figure this out, riders came up on us. "Where did you get those turnips?" I almost jumped out of my skin when I heard it. I knew they were the King's men because they wore such fancy clothes.

"Where did you get those turnips?"

"In the road"

They all laughed, slapped each other's shoulders. One got off his horse and pulled up an imaginary turnip. "See, turnips grow right out of the road." They all laughed. It was true that we both had red hair and little skinny bodies, but it was none of our doing, and there was no call for them to make fun of us. Even though I had a small body, someday I'd show them.

Two men dismounted and pushed our hands behind our backs so hard Mary cried out. When they tied our hands they twisted the rope so hard our hands got numb. Then they tied a lead rope to the ropes that tied our hands and started the long march toward London.

As we marched, Mary and I had time to talk. "Why don't you know where you came from or where you were going?" I asked.

"Well," she said, "it is a long story, but I'll tell it to you. It would be the first I ever said it all. My first remembering begins a long time ago when my mother took me to this big house on a road they called Kenton Way. She said she didn't have any place for me to sleep anymore so I was supposed to stay in this big house, and I was to do everything the lady told me. The name of the person who owned the house was Lady Stewart. She gave my mother some money, and I never saw my mother again. Lady Stewart bid me come in and follow her up two flights of stairs. Back then, that big space was frightening. When I looked down the stairs I felt dizzy and a strange smell stung my eyes and almost made me vomit. We were near the roof when she opened a door to a room that was about the same size as our house down on the river. She pointed to a small bed and told me to put my coat on it as that was where I was to sleep. She then took me down to the kitchen and told me that I was to do whatever the cook told me. Cook looked at me and said, 'That girl is too spindly to be eight years old; must be more like five.' Lady Stewart said, 'She'll grow'.

I cleaned and sewed everyday all day and never ever went outside the house. I was always looking out the windows wondering what it was like out there. If I looked out too long, someone would scold me because I was shirking my duty to the lady who was providing me with food and bed.

"I learned my numbers and how to measure things and to sew. I think I was seventeen years old when they told me Lady Stewart had died. I stayed in my room and peeked out from time to time at the people rushing around carrying all the furniture, rugs and pictures outside and loading them in wagons. Suddenly they opened the door. Two men grabbed my bed, my spare clothing and started down stairs. I tried to get my clothes but only got my coat. Some one pointed at me and said, 'Who is that?'

'A cleaning wench,' someone replied.'

A lady looked at me and said, 'She is too small and sickly to do any work. I don't want her. Send her down the road.'

"A man took my shoulder, turned me around, pointed me down the road and gave me a slight shove. 'Don't come back here or you'll go to jail.'

"That was a fortnight ago."

Tears began rolling down her cheeks and she said, "What will they do to us?"

I wanted to put my arms around her but couldn't, so I moved close enough to her to rub shoulders. We walked for several steps that way. She looked at me and smiled. She had enticed me, but I felt good about it.

I could understand Mary's feelings about being lost without a past or a future. If I were honest with myself, I would admit that I felt the same as she did. I didn't know where I came from or where I was going. I wanted to tell Mary about my life, but I stuttered when I told her that I hadn't had it so good either.

"It was up in Yorkshire. My mother and I lived in a shed near a town when I first remembered things. We had an iron stove that I remember well, for it was my job to go out each day and bring back pieces of coal in a bag and put it in the corner of our shed. Then at night, when my mother came home to cook and get warm, we would have fuel. Stealing coal was a job that taught me about people and what makes them think and do what they do.

"My mother told me that my father was Scottish and his name was Crinan. So she called me Crinan. But she never told me his surname. So I told everyone that my last name was Carter, which was my mother's surname.

"Then one night, although I had built a fire in the stove, she didn't come home and I had to cook a pot of food that had already been prepared. The next night she didn't come home either and although I still had food, I cried all night. The next day I went looking for her. She spent each day working someplace, but I did not know where.

"Many days passed and I had to find food. At first I would hide near a barn or a pigsty and after the person who fed the cows or pigs left I would creep in and steal the animal's food. I cooked the grain and added the pig food that often included the food that was spoiled or food from people's dishes they didn't want to eat.

"I wondered why grown people didn't chase and throw rocks at other children my size like they did me. I had noticed that other children wore cleaner clothes than I did. Maybe I needed cleaner clothes. I walked behind the houses and saw the clean clothes that might fit me

"I waited until after dark before I took them from the fence or from a rope that was hung in their yard. When my clothes got dirty, I would get some clean ones and put the dirty ones back where I had gotten them. I could now walk down a road without grown men throwing rocks at me.

"This gave me many more opportunities. I needed some shoes so I started looking for shoes setting outside drying. I crawled over a wall and was taking a pair from a rear step when a door opened and a women saw me and screamed, 'Thief, thief, catch that thief'.

"With shoes in hand I scrambled over the wall. Soon there were three men chasing me. They were gaining on me when I remembered an old well in some bushes where I had played when I was younger. I ducked behind the bushes and crawled down in the well and stayed until night. The men never even looked in the well.

"Whoever had been chasing me saw me clearly and if they ever saw me again they would remember me. I would have to go to another town where no one knew me. I went back to my shed got my clothes and a pot and started walking down the road toward the sun.

"It has been like that all my life, staying in one town until they suspect me of theft, then I would have to move on. Only once did they catch me.

"I stayed in jail for some time where I got to know several other people. But I didn't like them because they were always hitting me and taking my food."

Mary looked at me with tears in her eyes and moved toward me until our shoulders touched and we walked several steps that way.

In that short time we had become special to each other. She was so honest and didn't hold back anything. That meant she trusted me. I knew they would put us in separate jails and I might lose track of her.

" Maybe we can arrange to meet when we get out of jail so we don't lose each other," I suggested. She smiled as tears made her big blue eyes shine, and nodded.

"All right" I said, " Who ever gets out first will go every day and feed the pigeons at the bridge across the Thames." She nodded her head again and I knew we had a deal.

We had stopped near a tall wooden gate. The leader of the Kings Men shouted, "By order of His Majesty the King, open this gate for two prisoners." I heard latches and the gate swung wide and the horsemen herded us into the pen like sheep.

"What are your names?" the Jailer asked.

"She is Mary O'Kane and my name is Crinan Carter," I said.

The jailer pushed us into the pen and closed the gate and I heard the lock fasten.

The crowded jail looked like a pigpen with mud holes and from a corner where people did their personal things and the water washed it down into the sleeping area. It had been raining off and on for several days and since there was no roof, it was like a hog wallow. Right off, it started raining again. Mary and I huddled together as close as we could to stay warm.

'What'll they do to us?" Mary asked.

"They'll give us a year in the workhouse, then turn us loose."

"Then what'll we do?"

"Maybe we could get together and go to the Colonies in America. I hear there's work

there for the likes of us. And if we worked hard enough, we could start our own family." I didn't really believe what I said but I said it anyway. I heard myself say "We."

She said, "You mean you and me?"

I squeezed her hand and said, "Remember whichever one gets out first must go to the bridge every day at sundown."

We waited two days in the pen before a guard pushed us into a room where there was a judge sitting on a high bench. Looked like a pheasant with a white topknot. He said, "Tell me your names and who you work for. Don't lie or it will be bad for you."

"My name is Crinan Carter. I don't have a job."

"I'm Mary O'Kane. My mistress died and I have no place to live."

The Judge studied some papers, wrote something on them and said, "The Kings men saw you both steal turnips; therefore, you are both charged and convicted of theft and vagrancy. You will be shipped to the King's prison in the American Colony called Georgia where you will serve three years at hard labor." He waved us away like he was flicking dirt from his robe and a guard shoved us out the door.

I hugged Mary and said, "We'll be in America when we get out." Mary took a deep breath and whispered, "Maybe we could have our own house with linens and fine furniture and our own family."

Next morning a group of soldiers ordered the women to line up against a wall where they tied their hands together with small ropes then tied the small rope to a hawser. But Mary refused to join the others against the wall. A soldier grabbed her wrist but she wouldn't let go of my coat. The soldier struck her hand with a baton. Mary cried out and collapsed.

They tied her unconscious body to the hawser and dragged it through the mud and out the gate. I vowed that one day such men would be punished for their cruelty. Later they marched us men prisoners to a ship docked on the south bank of the Thames and loaded us into the forward hull where iron bars separated us from the women in the aft hull. Except for when the hatch on deck was open, it was stark black no matter whether it was day or night. I was cold all the time and it was so crowded I had to sleep in a crouched position. Although we had a bucket to relieve ourselves, it often ran over because it was seldom emptied and the stench caused my eyes to water.

Once when the hatch on deck was open, the sun shined forward into the women's side and I saw Mary. I shouted, "Mary O' Kane, I am Crinan. Meet me at the bars on the starboard side." I struggled through the wad of bodies, unkind language and an occasional cuffing or a kick. I could see Mary and I reached my hand through the bars and rubbed her cheek. We stayed together near the bars for the rest of the trip except for when we went for food and other things.

Even though we didn't know anything about Georgia, we were sure it would be better than England. We talked and planned about all we might do when we got out.

I had heard that the land extended west forever and that you could get as much as you wanted for free. They told us it was always warm and that you could grow anything you planted. Together we dreamed that we would build a large white two-story house with flowers and a large garden and next to the house a fine carriage house that held a large carriage and two buggies. We even got into the details of the rooms that included an attached toilet. All the pictures of our future life were in our minds and before we knew it, our voyage was over and we began our long march to the prison in a heat we had never experienced in England.

Two old men who had become ill during the voyage died from the heat. Their bodies weren't buried. They just threw them in the swamp.

Every day for three years, we marched to work where we built roads and bridges for the plantation owners. During the heat of summer, some of the weaker prisoners would die from the heat. I was always afraid that I too, might die from the heat and Mary would be alone when she got out.

Sometimes I got lucky and saw Mary on the women's side of the yard. We would wave to each, other but we were too far apart to talk. I kept daydreaming about getting out of prison in three years and taking Mary with me to the wilderness where we would find a place to build a home. I knew it was impossible, but it was this dreaming and planning that made the time pass.

Although I had learned how many days in a month and in a year, I couldn't keep track of how much more time I had left. Some of the others in prison knew about time and kept track of it with marks. I would ask them every so often how many days I had left. They were telling me I still had many days yet to serve when the jailor told me I was to leave that afternoon. I had become accustomed to the routine and hardship of prison. Now, they were going to turn me out into a strange country where there were savages who scalped people, snakes that bite people who died a few hours later. I was frightened and felt like asking the jailer if I could stay.

I didn't have much time to think, because a few hours later, those of us to be released were ordered double time to the gate, like we had some emergency and work that had to be done quickly. They gave us a speech about how we must obey the law, and a religious kind of person told us about Jesus and Hell. I'd heard all that stuff before. They were just telling us lies so we would do what they wanted.

As we passed through the gate, they gave us a blanket and two bags, one with corn and one with peas. I didn't want to leave with the other prisoners as they were a rowdy bunch, just looking' to get in more trouble. I wanted to find Mary so we could do what we planned. She had to serve the same amount of time as I did, so why hadn't they let her out at the same time as they did me? I saw no women let out that day. I would wait right near the gate until they released her.

That night I slept in the thick undergrowth close enough to the front prison gate to see anyone who came out. The next morning I saw women coming through the gate but there was no Mary. I hoped she hadn't died or was too sick to leave. I was disappointed but I was determined to wait until she was released.

Just before noon, from my perch high on the hillside, I saw the gate open and a lonely figure that looked like a small child pushed out. It carried a blanket and two bags as it walked slowly up the road. I was curious, so I walked closer until I could see it was Mary. I raced after her and caught her as she started down the road to no place. We hugged and I kissed her cheek. We sat down and talked a while, then she said, "Where are we going to sleep tonight?"

"We'll just find a nest in some bushes and sleep close together to keep warm."

"We can't sleep together we're not married."

I hadn't thought that Mary would be so proper but I liked it better than the girls I had known who didn't care about anything.

As we walked along the road, not knowing where it led or what we would do when we got to where it led, I was thinking about what she said. I didn't want to be separated from Mary again. That meant we'd have to get married. I really didn't know how you did it, but I knew that you had to go before a preacher. I guessed a preacher would know what to do.

So right then and there I took both Mary's hands, looked into those big blue eyes and said, "Will you marry me and be my wife?"

"Surely, you're going to need some help on this land you're going to get and I haven't anything to do I'd like better than help build us a place of our own. Where are we going to get married?"

"We're coming to the village I saw when we were working on the Alexander Plantation road. It's just around the corner."

It was early afternoon and many people were out and about. Mary spied a lady in her yard hanging up clothes and said, "You stay here cause that lady might be frightened if a man comes in her yard. I'll go ask her where there's a minister."

Mary came back with the directions. But while she was gone I had spied a Smithy at his anvil. A man had to have a ring so I asked the Smith if I could have a used horseshoe nail. He handed me one. Using two stones I bent the nail around a twig the size of Mary's finger.

We found the Preacher, but when we asked him to marry us, he looked at us in our prison clothes. I could tell he was about to refuse us. We had no coins to give him. "You may as well marry us 'cause we're going to stay together anyway," Mary said, "You wouldn't want to be the cause of making us commit adultery, would you?"

The Preacher must have decided to marry us rather than be a party to adultery. He took us into his house and called his wife into the room to hear him say his words. I put my ring on Mary's finger and he said we were man and wife. That sounded real respectable.

Then he opened a big book and wrote our names in it. I stared at the marks that were my name, Crinan Carter. I asked him which was Mary's marks and which were mine. He pointed to some of the marks and said, "This one is yours." He also gave us a piece of paper that had our name marks on it. That was the first time I had ever seen my name marks. Mary and I felt like real people with our name marks in the big book and the paper that said we were man and wife.

I remembered that the Alexander Plantation had a rocky hillside covered with brambles. It had never been farmed. There on the hill, under a blackberry bush, we made our nuptial bed.

As we snuggled together Mary said, "We are a family, aren't we? We aren't just friends, we belong to each other, don't we?"

I could feel what she meant. For the first time in my life I felt like a real person. I wondered why being married to Mary made me feel that I was legitimate person.

" Yes," I said, "It is just the beginning of a real family with children and grand children. We'll have lots of people who will own us and we will own them.

We called the hill "Drum," the name of the castle in Scotland where my mother said my father was born. We didn't realize then that we would be sleeping on that hill for years to come.

CHAPTER II

IT WAS A START

THAT NIGHT WE HUDDLED TOGETHER on a mattress of leaves and our blankets to keep us warm in an early spring fog. I tried to sleep, but I was so excited my mind wouldn't settle down. I felt as if I had just been born and was beginning life. And there was Mary, cuddled up to me like a baby, the only person who had ever liked me. We would work together like a team of horses and build a home and start a family. I knew we could do it.

As soon as it got light enough, I eased myself out of Mary's arms, climbed to the top of the hill where we had slept and began examining it. Yes, there were stones but they were loose and you could stack them in a pile. The soil was better than what I had seen in Yorkshire. The only problem was the blackberry brambles, which probably was the reason Old Man Alexander hadn't tried to farm it. But I remembered how the owners of the land in Yorkshire had destroyed the brambles that crowded out everything they planted.

I was thinking that this hill was part of the Alexander Plantation and if they had no use for the land, the old man might rent it in exchange for part of the crop, like they did in Yorkshire.

Mary was just beginning to awaken when I returned. I reached down and took her tiny hand in mine and said, "Would you like to live on this hill if we build a shelter and a fireplace? It wouldn't be much, but it would be ours."

"How will you buy it?" she said.

I explained that we would make a handshake agreement to farm the hill and give half of everything we grew to Alexander if he allowed us to live on the hill and work the land, just like everyone in Yorkshire does.

She abruptly stood up, threw her arms around me and hugged me. I knew that meant, "yes."

We were anxious about talking to Alexander for neither of us had ever talked to a landowner as an equal person. We had only taken orders from them. We had seen poor common people who had presumed to be equal to landowners flogged for that presumption.

Holding hands and our breath, we walked down to the big house where we found the old man, Alexander, inspecting his flowers.

" Good morning! Are you Mr. Alexander who owns this plantation?"

" That's me. What is your business here?"

His answer was short and blunt, but you could see a kindness in his eyes that gave me the confidents to proposition my superior as if we were equals.

"We've come to ask you if we could farm that hill there with the stones and brambles."

He chuckled, "Go ahead but you'll have to give half of everything you grow to me."

You could see that he didn't believe we could farm it and whatever effort we put into it would just make the land more valuable.

That very day Mary and I went to that hill and with our bare hands started taking rocks from the hill. It was hard work but it felt so good we continued working even though we were so hungry we felt weak.

We had enough beans, peas and corn from the bags they gave us when we got out of prison to feed us for quite a while but in the excitement of having our own land to farm we had forgotten to think how we would cook it without a pot and utensils. Maybe we could borrow what we needed until we could get our own.

I felt more comfortable around poor people than with rich folks so I walked down to the

slave shed to see what I could borrow. I couldn't see anyone around, though it was obvious that people lived there. I heard someone singing in a soft voice and went to see who it was. An old Negro woman was busy slicing vegetables into a boiling pot. She was so engrossed in her work that I startled her when I said, "I'm camping up on that hill with all the brambles on it. Mr. Alexander has rented it to us. We have beans, peas and corn but we have no pots to put them in and no spoons to ladle them. We thought perhaps you had a spare pot and spoons we could borrow for a short while. She immediately started rummaging through a closet of old pots and wooden bowls.

"You got yourself a job trying to clear off them brambles so you can plant" she said.

She handed us a pot, two bowls, two spoons, a knife and handed me a firebrand from her cooking fire. "You are just borrowing these and if that House Nigger wants to know where these things went, I'll tell him you borrowed them and that you'll bring them back directly."

She seemed proud to be able to help us. One day I would pay her for her kindness.

Ain't no man so big and strong that he can claim that all his success, accomplishments and treasure are all his doings. He is only fooling himself if he thinks so and is a fraud if he acts so. His pride blinds him to the truth. It was the Smithy who must be credited the most for our success. He gave us the right kind of help at the right time to make us successful.

Any person in that part of Georgia who wanted something created from metal had no choice but to ask the Smithy and no matter their wealth or position, they had to ask him politely to use his talents. As the only Smithy in those parts, he came to know the business of everyone within twenty miles of his shop. When we needed to work for coin, he knew who needed tasks done and could pay for it. He would tell us about them.

Mary picked berries and traded them for ground wheat to make bread. Sometimes the big house needed an expert seamstress like Mary. They often paid her in coin.

We finally had enough money to buy a pick, a shovel, a hammer and an ax. Then we made a sledge that we loaded with stones and together we pulled it to the boundary of our rented property and stacked the stones. We rolled the large boulders to the border as foundation for a stone fence we built around our little hill.

Together, Mary and I planned where we would build our shelter. We would build it at the top of the hill so it would drain well and not too far from the stream where we could get water.

We began our cabin by gathering the right size stones and sticking them together with mud. In this way, we a built a fireplace.

Everyone said we were just wasting our time, for even if we cleared off the brambles they would just grow back before we could plant anything. But I knew how to get rid of those thorny bushes. I had seen it done in Yorkshire.

The Smithy told us about our neighbor, who raised goats and used the milk to make Cheese, that he sold to ship captains provisioning for a voyage. But he was lame, and often needed help. He was happy to trade us goat milk for our help. When we offered to take those kids who needed weaning and pasture them inside the stone fence we had built, he gave us a quart of milk a day.

But we had an additional reason for keeping the goats. I had seen what goats did in Yorkshire. The kids could spot any green sprout that had the audacity to grow from roots after we had cut them. The kids would chomp those delicious tender roots every time they showed themselves. Yet there were roots deep under ground that would wait till spring to come up when there were no goats.

Old Alexander's favorite food was pork and it was for this reason that the primary livestock on his plantation was pigs. Each year, his four sows raised a couple litters. This meant that each spring and each fall he had about thirty-five pigs to wean and fatten. That required a lot of work and feed. When I offered to care and feed two litters of pigs until they were weaned, he offered us one of the piglets for that service.

As we chopped and cleared the brambles, the goats chewed of any sprout that had the audacity to try to grow. The pigs rooted down in the loose soil I had made when I took out the brambles with the pick and shovel. They loved the tender roots and none were left to come up in the spring.

By the end of the summer, our hill was free of brambles and as I had seen in Yorkshire. The brambles would not grow again unless the land was left fallow for several years.

Late summer came, and we were still camping out on the hill. Winter would come soon with its cold rain, and we would need shelter. We had already built a fireplace and a chimney, but we would have to build a shelter next to the fireplace to keep us warm.

For much of the time that summer, Mary and I hired out and by early fall we had saved five pounds. The money looked pretty, but it was time to spend it. We asked the Smithy how much he would charge for a long saw and a drawknife. He said, " Five pounds six pence."

"But we only have five pounds," I said, "We need the tools to build a shelter."

He was a bachelor and spent most of his time in his shop. In his deliberate and slow speech, he said, "You can make up for the six pence if your wife will clean the two rooms where I live and hang curtains on the four windows."

It took one day for Mary and I to clean up his rooms and Mary sewed his curtains from the fabric he provided. We picked up the tools we had bargained for that evening.

The next day, I began cutting logs in the thick pine forest behind our hill, while Mary removed the limbs with a hatchet she had borrowed from the slave shed.

Together Mary and I drug one of the logs to a flat spot on top of the hill where we intended building our shelter for the winter. It had taken us what I thought was a good part of a day, and we were dead tired. Mary exclaimed, "We'll never get our shelter made if it takes as long as that to just get one log in place." I knew she was right.

I went to the big house and knocked on the door. Justice, Alexander's house slave, as always, answered the door. I told him I wanted to talk some business with Squire Alexander. He asked me to wait while he consulted his master. He returned and beckoned me enter and led me into what I took to be a parlor. It was quite large and the walls were so covered with paintings, drapes and tapestries I couldn't tell from what material the walls were made.

Alexander rose and shook my hand and bid me sit and state my business. I explained that I needed to build a shelter for the winter and that I was cutting some trees in the Oglethorpe forest to build it but that it was too far to drag the logs by hand and I needed a mule. "If he would lend me the mule I will drag enough dead wood from the forest to his wood yard to last him for the winter.

He didn't say yes or no, instead he said, " Ask Kelly in the shed which is the best mule for dragging timber." I wouldn't forget his kindness.

We notched the ends of the logs where they met at the corners deep enough so that most of the logs touched each other all along their full length and left only tiny cracks between them. There was an opening for an entrance and a window on the south side. It was all attached to the hearth and chimney we had been building all summer. Since the logs were not perfectly straight we pounded wood chips and slivers in the spaces between logs and sealed the small holes with mud. We had bought some crocks at an estate sale that we no longer needed. We traded them to the Lower Creek Indians for twenty deer hides that we used to cover our roof. We tied long strips of willows tightly together to cover our doorway. Our bed was strips of cowhide stretched across a frame of pine poles on legs of thick pine stumps. We slept between two blankets and bearskins I had traded for from the Upper Creek Indians who lived near by. We were so proud of our bed that the first night we slept in it, we stayed in it till the sun was high in sky. But we didn't sleep all that time. We felt as if we were on top of the world. Our first child was born of love not of lust.

Throughout the winter we enjoyed our cozy one room and though our floor was pounded earth, Mary kept it very clean by sprinkling it with water and sweeping the loose dry dirt outside.

The next spring not one bramble sprouted. We bought seed from old Man Alexander and even though Mary's stomach had gotten big with our first child she still helped plant the white potatoes, beans, corn and sweet potatoes. Everything we planted was growing and I was sure we would have enough to eat and some to sell for coin that we could use to buy things we needed at the store.

Mary was doing just fine until in the middle of the night, on what they told me was June 26, 1769, when she woke up crying and screaming. I had been foolish, to expect such a little girl to birth a baby. I felt guilty for expecting too much of Mary.

I was out of breath when I pounded on Old Man Alexander's door. Justice opened the door. I shouted out, " Mary is trying to have a baby but she is too small and she'll die unless a doctor can help. I must find a Doctor."

"You best get Sheli right away. She is the best mid-wife in this county. She'll get you a baby. She is in the shed."

I went to Sheli's kitchen door and shouted, "My wife is trying to birth but she is too small and she needs help." Everyone in the shed must have awakened cause candles were lit everywhere.

Sheli came through the shed opening and said, "Where is she?"

"She in our cabin up on the hill." I shouted.

"You get right up there and build a big fire, fill your biggest kettle with water and put it on that fire. I'll be up directly. I must get some clean cloth to put in that water. Just don't you fret; we'll get that baby out."

Well it took all night but she got that kid out and Mary was just fine. This was the second time this tall, smart and kindly Negro had come to our rescue. I was indebted to her and I would later have a chance to repay her for the kindness that was in her soul.

We called our son, Eric. He didn't look like much when he was first born. He had no hair and was wrinkled and red, but in less than a year, he was walking and getting into trouble.

We farmed that hill and gave half of everything we grew to Alexander. But each year we did better than the year before, and we were buying new tools, a team of oxen, some cows, pigs and a riding horse. The wagon we bought from the Smithy was the best of its kind.

But I was very careful not to make Mary with child again for I could not take a chance of losing her. I could not think of a life without her.

As soon as Eric could walk, we taught him to work just like we did. We were proud. When we talked to friends, it was always Eric does this and Eric does that. Things were going good for us, but as I look back on it now I should have known it wouldn't last forever.

The three of us had worked in the hot Georgia sun since dawn. When dusk came, we did our chores. Eric milked the cow, I unhitched and fed the oxen and Mary began fixing supper.

Eric was so tired he could hardly sit straight at the table and needed wood chips to prop his eyelids open. He said he was thinking about how good it would feel to go swimming tomorrow. Then he fell asleep and his face fell in his plate. He woke up quickly for his face had fallen in the gravy. I couldn't stop laughing.

Chapter III
The Road To Success Is Never Smooth Or Easy

It was Sunday. Mary and Eric went to church as every white person was expected to do. But I always stayed home and did chores like sharpening the scythe or fixing the sledge.

Ever since it had gotten warm, after Eric got out of church, he ran down to the slave quarters to get Dobi and the two of them would go swimming.

Dobi lived with his mother, Sheli, who helped bring Eric into this world. All the slaves lived in a big shed with partitions that separated the bedrolls of each family. Everybody ate the food Sheli cooked and served on a long table.

Except for the house slaves and Sheli, all the slaves worked in Old Man Alexander's fields and would not have had the time to do household chores for their family. It was more efficient to have a common household. Alexander had Sheli to do the cooking, maintain the quarters and be the wise and soothing mother to all the workers. Her wisdom and concern for all humans kept the morale of the slaves at an even keel.

Dobi and Eric were the only children living on the Alexander plantation except for the children living in the big house. But they weren't allowed to talk to Dobi and Eric.

Eric asked me why they couldn't play with him and Dobi. I explained that since he and Dobi couldn't read and didn't own any land, Alexander's people thought their children would learn bad things from them.

Dobi was a lot taller than Eric with long brown arms and legs. He could run like the wind and jump like an antelope. We thought Dobi was at least two years older than Eric for he was walking when we first arrived at the plantation.

We all liked Dobi because he kept everyone laughing at his jokes, his funny faces and the way he playfully mocked pompous adults. Eric and Dobi didn't get to be together much because they both had to work in the fields from early morning till dark.

It was a warm Sunday and right after church, Eric went to the slave shed to see Dobi, whose mother was at the outside fireplace making lard by cooking pork fat in a big iron pot. She wiped the sweat from her forehead with the tail of her apron and handed Eric some cracklings that had already drained and cooled. She knew he liked them.

I was down at the end of my field near the quarters when I heard her say, "Master Alexander took Dobi to town, I don't reckon I know when they'll be back."

Instead of going swimming, Eric spied on the plantation kids. He said they didn't look very strong, even though someone was always giving them something to eat or drank. And with all the scolding the adults gave them, it was no wonder they didn't laugh. They just pouted.

Later that afternoon Eric went down to the slave shed to see if Dobi was back yet. Dobi saw Eric before he got to the shed and yelled, "Let's go swimming."

I heard Eric say, "It'll be dark pretty soon."

"It's fun to swim at night," Dobi shouted.

They raced to the river, climbed to the top of the cypress tree that hung over the river. I heard them hit the water and then some giggling. Even though it was getting dark, they swam until they were exhausted. On the way back, I saw Dobi pick up a stick and while he was hobbling around like old Alexander in the dark, he slipped and fell in a mud hole. As he was getting upright with his face covered with mud, he raised his hand over his head, pointing his finger at the sky, shouted in old Alexander's voice,

"Whoever put that mud hole in my path shall receive fifty lashes." I laughed until my sides hurt.

The next Sunday after church, Eric went to the slave shed to get Dobi. He returned with a long sad face. He said Dobi 's mother was staring into the flames of the outside fireplace. He said, "that when he asked where Dobi was, she said, "Master Alexander done sold him at the auction."

Eric asked her why she couldn't visit him.

Sheli told him that the master didn't know who bought him and she guessed she would never see her baby anymore.

Eric told her that Dobi knew where we lived so he could come see us.

Sheli told Eric that most masters watch young men real close after they wean 'em from their mama, cause they get lonesome and run away. Dobi's mother started crying. Eric said he was embarrassed and left.

I told Eric that the new owner would probably take good care of Dobi because a strong boy like Dobi was valuable.

Eric thought for a while and then said, "But Papa, why are all the Negroes slaves?"

"Because they are prisoners from another country."

"You and Mama were prisoners when they brought you to the Georgia prison from England."

"We are white and white people can't be slaves."

"I don't understand. Mr. Waddle is white, sold his son in exchange for a span of oxen and a wagon. His son is a slave because he has to work and he can't leave."

"That's different. The father got something for his son's work and at the end of the time of the indenture the boy is free. Black slaves will never be free." I knew my answers to Eric's questions weren't good enough for him or me.

A few days later, when Eric went to do the evening milking, our cow was missing. He could see the hole in the fence where she had escaped so he followed her tracks into the forest. He hadn't gone far when a pebble hit him in the back. He quickly turned and there in the bush behind him was Dobi. Eric said he asked Dobi what he was doin' there.

Dobi said he ran away cause they whipped him for no reason. He showed Eric a raw gash across his cheek.

"What are you goin' to do?"

" I'm going' to live in the swamp where nobody can find me. I'm powerful hungry though. Ain't had nothing' to eat since yesterday forenoon."

"As soon as I find the cow, I'll get you some vittles."

Eric was driving the old Jersey back to the corral when he saw two men on horseback dragging Dobi behind them. His head was bleeding. Eric asked me, "Why did they have to hurt him?"

Eric was mad and told me that when he grew up, he would get revenge on the Wallace Clan for what they did to Dobi. I told him, " It's none of our affair. They bought and paid for Dobi and they can do anything they want to him."

A week later we saw a man from the Wallace Clan leading a mule with Dobi tied to its back. Dobi wasn't moving. We were worried and followed the Wallaces to the big house.

Old Alexander saw them and hobbled out on the veranda to see what they wanted. Jackson Wallace said, "You didn't tell us what a hard case this one was. He has run away three times. We want our money back."

While Jackson Wallace was talking to Alexander, Dobi's mother was trying to wake him up. George Wallace saw her and struck her with a quirt.

"You leave that woman alone or I'll have you whipped. She's my property," Alexander said. "Furthermore, you bought that boy and he's yours to keep. If you want to damage your own property, that's your business but I'm not taking him back." The Wallace family was so mean they scared Eric, and he ran back to our house ahead of me.

We didn't have much time to feel indignant about Dobi's plight. Alexander summoned me to his parlor where he explained that two English generals named Sir George Prevost and Robert Howe had invaded Georgia, captured Savannah and was heading toward Augusta. Not only that, but a bunch of Indians and people from Florida had been hired by the English to steal, murder and burn houses of the Georgia people if they were not loyal to England.

Old Man Alexander told me it was my duty to join Nathan Green to run the English out of Georgia. He said it wouldn't take more than a month since the English didn't know how to fight Georgia style. I told him

I couldn't leave Mary and Eric. But he told me he would take care of my family. He also said that he wouldn't want anyone living on his place if they weren't willing to protect their home and friends. He said that if his son were not in France, he would send him.

I knew it would be difficult to tell Mary and Eric that I would have to go with Nathan Green. I explained to Mary everything Alexander had told me, including that he promised to take care of her and Eric while I was gone. I told her it was not just because I didn't like the way England had treated us, but because I wanted to do what Alexander wanted me to do. Alexander was such a good man. And besides, if we didn't drive the English out they might destroy our home and take us back to England.

That night we gathered everything we thought I would need plus the things Alexander sent over. He sent a special bedroll, a musket, a pistol, a sword, a dagger, powder and balls. The next morning a bunch of men came by our house in some wagons. I kissed Mary, shook Eric's hand and told him to take care of his mama. Then I got in the wagon that headed down the swamp road to the camp where I was to learn and train to be a soldier.

I kept looking back and waving to Mary and Eric until they were out of sight. I felt uneasy and almost jumped off the wagon. I had a feeling, even though it made no sense, that they would need me and I wouldn't be there. But Alexander had promised to take care of them and I trusted him. As it turned out, my feelings were right.

A few days later after I left for training, Mary and Eric scythed all the meadow grass. And a day or two after that Mary was loading the hay on the sledge and Joe and Pete, our oxen were hauling it up to Eric who was up on top of a pile of hay building a haystack that would shed rain like a thatched roof, when he saw Dobi running toward him. Somewhere in the trees dogs were yelping and howling as they followed Dobi's scent. Eric knew if those dogs caught Dobi, they would tear him to bits. He motioned him to come to the haystack. Eric dug a hole in the top of the haystack, Dobi crawled in the hole and Eric covered him up just as the yelping dogs, Wallace and his sons came running across the field.

The dogs started milling around the stack, sniffing and barking. Jackson Wallace rode up to the haystack and started tearing the haystack apart just as Mary got to the yard with a load of hay on the sledge. "Jackson Wallace,"

Mary said, "You get out of that stack yard before I tell Alexander what you doin' to his haystacks. He'll have you whipped."

"If you are hiding that runaway, we'll string you up," Jackson said. He called off his noisy sniffing dogs and rode toward the big house.

Eric was afraid that Jackson would tell Old Alexander that they were hiding Dobi, and they'd be in trouble.

That night, Mary saw that Eric was upset about something. Later he asked what they would do to a person, who hide a run-away? Mary told him that they could and would hang them.

The wagon that picked up me and a half dozen other men only took a half of a day to get to the training camp where we would be trained in the use of guns, knives and other things.

A couple days later, while we were doing target practice, I was surprised to see Dobi running through the woods toward the captain's tent. I could hear him asking for Mr. Papa.

I hurried over to the Captain to explain who this negro boy was and that he probably had a message from my family. I was fearful that something had happened to them so I hurried him out of hearing distance of the others. "What is your message? What has happened?"

"They all right, Mr. Papa."

'Then why are you here?"

"The Red coats, they are goin' to attack the Alexander Plantation."

"How do you know?

"I hid from Mr. Wallace in your haystack until everybody went to sleep. Then Eric haltered your horse Tobins. We both got on him bareback and road him into the swamps.

Eric said no one could see us, and dogs couldn't smell us because we were on the horse and all they would smell was the horse. We would find a place in the swamp for me to hide. He had some corn bread for me to eat. But we had to be very careful, cause if they found out Eric was helping me escape, they would hang both of us. We found the old Indian house in the swamp that I knew about and sat there for a while. Eric told me that his papa was a soldier and was going to fight that English general and his Redcoats who were robbing people and burning their houses. He said you were learning to be a soldier over on the north flats."

I asked what Redcoats did to slaves. Eric thought they did the same to slaves as they did to everyone else. They shoot them.

I was getting impatient. "Dobi, please tell me how you know the Redcoats are going to attack the Alexander place."

Dobi continued, "I have to tell it all like it was so you can understand, then you will believe me."

Dobi kept on talking. He said Eric needed to get home, so he left the bag of sweet potatoes and cornbread and promised to bring more food on Sunday.

"After dark, Eric went to the slave shed where my mother was sick in bed and whispered in her ear that I had found a place to hide and that he was going to bring me some food the next day. Eric told me that she grabbed him and hugged him so hard he couldn't breath.

"The next day when Eric brought my food, he didn't ride Tobins cause people would be curious and get suspicious.

"We were sitting in front of the Indian place, listening to the noisy birds while I was eating mama's vittles when we heard a loud boom. Then another boom caused dead branches to fall on our heads. We looked up and there, not more than twenty paces away, was Jackson Wallace riding on a boat paddled by two slaves. He was pointing a musket at me. I ducked under the hut and Eric followed. We crawled through a lot of vines until we were sure Jackson had lost us. Then we started running across a clearing when Jackson Wallace jumped out in front of us with his guns ready. He stopped just long enough to say he wasn't going to catch us and bring us back alive, instead he was going to kill us and hang our carcass on the fence to show others what happens to run-a-ways and their friends. The time it took him to say those words was enough time for Eric and me to fall on the ground and Jackson missed.

"We zigzagged through the forest and Jackson kept firing as fast as his slaves could reload his muskets. We knew how long it took to reload so when Jackson was about to fire, we ducked behind a tree or fell in a ditch that caused him to miss.

"We had just hidden in some bushes to get a breath, when nearby we heard a voice say, 'Fire when ready!' A loud noise almost blew off my head and from the bushes we watched soldiers in red coats with knives on the end of their guns running toward the spot where Jackson Wallace had been. They stabbed and cut. Then we heard someone say, 'We got one rebel and two slaves. That Reb had a lot of cheek attacking a whole platoon. Don't bother burying them. Just hide their bodies. We got to get back to our platoon before we loot that Alexander plantation or we won't get our share. They lined up and marched away.

"Eric said they were the Redcoats and they were gonna attack our folks. I told Eric I knew where Mr. Papa was and I would run as fast as I could to tell you about the Red Coats.

Eric said he would run back and tell Mr. Alexander."

Dobi was right, he needed to tell me the whole story or I wouldn't have believed him. This meant that they would burn the buildings including my cabin, kill the people including my son and hurt the women including Mary.

Dobi and I ran to Nathan Green's camp. I told him what Dobi had told me and that if he couldn't help, Dobi and I would have to go to the Alexander Plantation to protect our families and our homes.

Both Nathan Green and Morgan were very interested in the news. And while I was there I heard them say that now they knew where at least some of the Redcoats would be and if they could catch them just right, as they were loading their muskets, they could destroy most of them. They could follow those Redcoats they didn't kill to Sir George Prevost's main army. Then Nathan could keep surprising the English main army, destroying their supplies and stop them from conquering Charleston port where the English army could get all the guns and powder they needed from their ships.

They talked about the whole country for a long time but I needed to leave at once. Mary and Eric needed me. "I must go now, I can't wait for you to decide," I said.

"We will all go right now and you will be the scout to lead us to the Alexander Plantation," Mr. Green said. "You will need all of us to protect your family from a company of redcoats. You have learned a scout's signals so you can warn us if they discover where we are. Since you know the ground near the Alexander Plantation, you must show us the best way to stay hidden until we make a surprise attack and scare the pee out of those we don't kill. Frightened soldiers usually don't take the time to reload when they are running for their lives. Be on your way. We'll be behind you. Just keep us posted."

"Yes," I said. "I will do as you say but I am leaving right now." I motioned to Dobi and we started down Swamp Road. We hadn't gone more than ten rods when we began hearing the whistles that assemble the men with muskets.

From time to time we stopped to rest and I would make a screech like an eagle. In a short time we would hear an eagle call from behind us.

We had traveled about half the distance to the plantation when we heard some talking. I crawled a tall pine tree so I could see who it was. Sure enough it was the men with guns and red uniforms that brought back many unhappy memories to me. I felt dread, fear and above all anger. By the time I got down to the ground, all my anger became resolve.

I cupped my hands around my mouth and made the sound of a crow. There was no answer. I tried again. No answer. How could I tell them the Redcoats were just ahead of us. We went back to the top of a hill and I tried again. Shortly I heard an eagle screech followed by a crow caw.

I told Dobi that I didn't know how we were going to know from which direction the redcoats would attack the plantation if we couldn't see which direction they were headed.

"If I catch up with them and walk behind them, they won't pay no mind to a black slave boy and I can let you know whether they will attack from the swamp or the hill," Dobi said. I thought about how this slave boy had proven himself to be very smart, as well as a person who was concerned for his friends and family.

"Yes," I said, "If they are attacking from the swamp, drop this willow staff across your path. If they are going to attack from the hill, lay this pine staff across your path.

The next evening, as I followed the swamp road I was delighted to find the pine staff in the middle of the road. I made my crow sound again and followed it with the magpie sound. I got an immediate crow and eagle sound in reply and ran back to the men in our army. I told Mr. Green that the red coats were fixing to attack from the hill where my wife and son lived. I also told him about the deep ravine behind the hill where they could hide until they were ready to surprise the redcoats as they were going down the hill to loot the plantation.

That night, I slipped into the plantation from the swamp. I climbed the tall pine that overhung our house but I kept my musket pointed at the doorway, just in case some Redcoat tried to go in our house.

That night, I had a hard time staying awake in that tree. Just as the sun came up, I heard a loud voice say, "Form up." Then from out of the woods behind our house, the Redcoats in three groups came marching down the hill. They ignored our cabin and began surrounding the big house. A volley was fired at the windows. But where were Green and his soldiers?

A loud blast of a horn almost caused me to jump out of my skin. I heard shouting coming from the forest behind our cabin. Muskets exploded as men poured past us, barking like dogs. I heard a Redcoat say, "It's that bloody Swamp Fox again." Like red ants fleeing a fire in their mound, the Redcoats dashed off in all directions.

Our soldiers didn't chase the Redcoats but instead began burying the English dead, and preparing their camp in our hayfield. I was watching them put up their tents when I saw Dobi coming toward our cabin. I went to meet him, took his arm and hustled him into my cabin and told Mary to keep Dobi inside until I got back. Then I walked over to Mr Green's camp, whose tent was in my hay field.

When I explained to him all that Dobi had done to help us and that he had done this, knowing full well, that if he were caught, he would probably be killed.

Green called his officers together and made a speech. All the officers contributed to a fund that I was to use to buy Dobi's freedom from the Wallace Clan. Mr. Green wrote out a bill of sale on paper for me. I bridled Tobins and rode to the Wallace rundown farm.

I had known such people in England and understood how their greed made them vulnerable to visible money so I showed about half of what I had. They jumped at the opportunity to get money and I was able to buy Dobi for half of what I had in contributions. I considered the balance as payment for caring for Dobi. Later I felt guilty, for Dobi was more a help than an expense.

The next morning I showed Dobi a piece of paper that Colonel Green said was a bill of sale for him. I told him all the Georgia soldiers had chipped in to buy his freedom. "Dobi" I said, " this means that I bought you from the Wallace Clan and you belong to me. You saved the plantation and I am giving you your freedom. But if you don't stay with us, someone will just make you a slave again. So you'll be like my son and live with us. While I'm away being a soldier, we'll need your help. I am sure you'll do your best"

Dobi's eyes were shining when he said, "Master Papa, I'll do my best and make you proud. Can I go tell mama what you said?"

"Go tell her, but be back here in the morning to start digging potatoes," I said."

CHAPTER IV

THE VICISSITUDES OF A SOLDIER FIGHTING FOR INDEPENDENCE

I WAS GLAD TO BE HOME even for a few hours, but I had to leave the next day. The worst part of leaving was when Mary cried. As I walked away, I put my hands over my face and sobbed quietly for I knew Mary would be lonely and frightened while I was gone and I would live in misery without her near me.

But I had made a promise and besides I didn't want to live in a country that was ruled by a king that treated poor people so badly.

Nathan Green was impressed by my scouting ability. He did not realize that all the time I was in England, I had been a scout for myself. If I had not learned to spy on other people without being discovered, I would not be alive today. They would have either executed me or I would have starved.

Nathan Green gave me a mule and a cart and told me to find out where Sir George Prevost's Redcoats were and what they were doing. I didn't have to ask why he took my musket and powder from me. If the Redcoats caught me with them, they would have suspected me of being a rebel spy.

I followed the tracks of the Redcoats who had attacked the plantation. They turned north and were soon joined by another group of tracks. Some of the new tracks appeared to be wearing Indian moccasins. I turned around and went back to the Georgia and Carolina men. It took half a day to reach them. I hadn't realized I had out distanced them so much.

I explained all I had seen. About how many were going north and how many wore moccasins. I was able to answer all of Nathan Green's questions.

They loaded me up with food supplies and gave me another mule for my cart. They would now follow close behind me and prepare a hit and run campaign that could cripple the British before they came in contact with the Colonial army.

I had traveled for only a couple days when I heard musket fire to the north. I crawled up a tree and was half way up when I saw a big fire. I signaled with one crow's call, an eagle's high voice and a screech owl's cry. Then I crawled down and caught my hobbled jenny who had stopped eating and had her ears cocked toward the musket firing.

I hitched up and headed toward the fire but stopped some distance away, tied up the mule and crawled up a tree so I could see better what was happening.

"Well, what do we have here," a voice said.

"It is a sorry mule, I would say," said another voice.

"That mule and cart is mine," I said. "I am looking to find the Kings army so as to earn some money hauling things for them. You look to be one of the King's Redcoats. Can you tell me where to find your general?"

"Well, we've something for you to haul. We won't be paying you but you'll be where you can talk to our supply officer. He is the one who hauls loot back to camp after we make a raid."

We went near the house and buildings that were burning. There was a pile of goods of all kinds including a lot of food. They loaded so much on my cart there was no room for me to sit. So I had to walk and lead the mule.

It was before noon when our road began moving up a ridge and some Redcoats stepped out and ordered me to stop. I guessed they intended taking the contents of my cart. The Redcoats who were behind me came forward and showed them some papers.

They motioned me to go on and shouted, "Hurry up, we need to reach headquarters before nightfall."

It was just after sundown when we topped the ridge overlooking a wide river valley that was covered with tents and campfires. There was so much movement that the valley looked like an ant colony. Some Redcoats were marching back and forth and some were unloading wagons and some were loading wagons. Horses were being unharnessed and fed.

We marched straight down into the valley through the tents to a space where wagons were circled and several large tents were pitched. I was directed to a tent where a redcoat told me where I was to unload my cart. After I unloaded I went to the tent and ask to see the supply officer to get employment hauling supplies.

A white headed old man came out to look at my mule and cart. "It won't haul a heavy load, but you can travel fast. We can use you to travel with our raiding parties. If you will return here the day after tomorrow, you may join our raiding parties as we start marching north. For each day you and your mule work, we will pay you six pence.

Even though it was nighttime, I traveled back the way I had come until I reached the Carolina and Georgia boys. Mr. Green was very excited about what I had seen. I was questioned about the details of everything I saw or heard.

I might not be able to write down on paper what I saw and what they said to me, but my mind could remember every detail because I paid attention.

It was decided that I would be employed by the English and would report back from time to time about their location and where they could be expected to attack.

I soon found out that there was another English Army running around Georgia. The General's name was Campbell, so I went to work for him cause it was closer to home and I knew the country better than in Carolina.

It was almost half a year that I worked for Campbell hauling his booty and telling Green or Morgan where to catch the Redcoats. Couple times they even attacked the main English army in Augusta. The English were trying to rule Georgia and collect taxes.

I had told Mary that I put my mark on a contract that required me to be in the war for two years. It was not so bad at first when we operated in Georgia, because I could come home often to see how Mary, Eric and Dobi were doing. But when everyone had to go north because the English were attacking Charleston I couldn't come home and I started worrying about my family. I knew I was worrying for no good reason. After all, they were safer than I was, but I couldn't stop worrying.

It was then they said that Mary started spending so much time looking out the window. She would awaken at dawn and stare at the horizon until the sun rose. I think she was trying to use her mind to bring me home. I knew she would do that so I convinced Cappy, an officer who had been educated in England, to write down what I said on paper so I could send it by a post rider that cost me all my pay. I sent it to the Alexander Plantation in Georgia. I was sure that Old Alexander would read it to my family and they would feel better.

As I was told later, when Old Alexander sent a message to Mary telling her she had a letter that had come by a post rider, Mary's mouth opened wide, and she almost fainted as she started out the door mumbling, "Something has happened to papa."

Eric told me that Alexander knew that mama couldn't read the letter so he met them at the door and had them come into his special room with all the pictures and rugs on the wall. When he read the letter, they said it didn't sound like me but everyone felt better. My letters said that I was all right and working in a safe place and I hoped to come home in the spring.

Every so often I sent a letter and I understand that when they got one it was always a special occasion and everyone would be in good spirits for several days.

But soon my job became so demanding and there was none in our group who could write. Later Eric told me that everyday, Mary would ask Old Alexander if he had any writing from me. He would shake his head. Then one day, when mama asked him that question, Old Alexander said, " The war hasn't been going too well for us lately. General Washington hasn't won a single battle and we have lost a lot of men." Mama went home and cried all night.

Nathan Greens Army tried to drive Cornwallis, the British general, out of the Carolinas but the Red coats out numbered Green's army and my detachment was forced to retreat into Georgia a few miles from our cabin.

Dobi and Eric were unhitching the oxen when I walked in. I didn't see Mary but I heard her scream, "Crinan Carter, what're you doin' here?"

Mary leapt into my arms. She was so light I carried her all the way back to the cabin, kissing her all the way.

I shook hands with Dobi and Eric and slapped their backs like I did my men friends in town. While I was gone, Dobi and Eric did all the fieldwork, like plowing, planting, cutting, and stacking hay. I was proud of what they had done.

"Come see how good the corn and sweet taters are doin'," Eric said, "And we got six weanling pigs and a heifer calf."

Dobi said, "You won't see a weed in that field."

I went with them and inspected everything on the place and told them how proud I was of them. Then I told them something that Dobi and Eric would talk about for the next year. But we could never have guessed what grief and hardship would come with what I proposed.

I said, " The men in Captain Green's Army say that the best land in America is on the banks of a big river in the West called the Mississippi. Lieutenant Drew said he saw corn there so tall you couldn't reach the top of the stock with your hoe. If we win the war they say a family could get all the land they wanted for the taking. Now, you two boys are big enough to run a farm by yourselves. As soon as the war is over, we'll head west to the Mississippi. When we get there, each one of us will fence off our own farm. With three farms all together, we can help each other. How does that sound to you?"

"I'd like to raise the fastest horses in the country, " Eric said.

Dobi's eyes got big and his mouth opened wide. "Would I have a farm of my own just like white folks?"

"Sure, you're free to own land just like Eric," I said, "The trip'll take three or four months, so we need to make sure the wagon is in good shape. I'll make some spare wheels out of some good cured oak. Wish we could buy another wagon."

We sat around the table eating grits, chitlins and collard greens and I told them how we raided the British supply wagons. I told them that we may have lost a few fights, but I was sure the Redcoats would be driven out of the colonies soon. I said, they can't kill every one in America and they don't know who is loyal and who is their enemy. But I'm not going back to fight,

I've done my bit. George Washington can win the war without me. We got a lot of work to do before we move west."

The next morning Captain Ross, the Commander of my company, and Old Man Alexander came to our cabin to see me. We all sat around the Big Oak Tree and argued. Captain Ross said, "You've got to stay with us. You're the best scout we have."

"But my family needs me," I said.

Finally Old Man Alexander said, "I think you'd better go. They're going to need all the help they can get. I'll take care of your family, and when you return, I'll give you fifty pounds. We all got to do the most we can, because if we don't win, life in the colonies won't be worth living."

I knew I couldn't go against Old Alexander 'cause he was a landowner. When I told Mary that I had to go back to war, Mary cried, and I told Dobi and Eric to go to the cow shed where their straw mattresses were. I wanted to talk to Mama.

Sitting on their beds, Dobi and Eric talked about how exciting it would be to go with me and fight the Redcoats. Eric was as tall as I was and Dobi was taller. I scoffed at their suggestion and told them that the best thing they could do was to grow a lot of food and make preparation for our long trip to the big river valley in the west. I told them that when I got back we would use the fifty pounds Old Man Alexander promised me to buy another wagon, a span of oxen and maybe some cows. Then we'd head west. I could tell that the boys were sincere when they promised me they would take care of everything, but they didn't know how hard it was going to be.

I went north with Morgan's Army as a scout, but it soon became clear that the people who lived in an area were the most logical people to get good information about the Redcoats. So what was I going to do? I had not been trained to fight in a military formation. Besides, I was too small to march in a squad of normal sized soldiers. So they gave me the job of hauling supplies. Eventually I was given the responsibility of hauling the valuables from the homes of loyalists to a place where they were sold and the money given to the army. The loyalists were people who were loyal to King George. The community treated them as traitors and most of them fled to Canada or south into French and Spanish Country.

I was sent with five wagons and four slaves to the vacated homes or businesses of the loyalists. Some people didn't realize that money was as important to the success of an army as its soldiers.

We heard that Washington's army, with the help of the French, was winning the war. But in spite of that, we were sent to a mansion that was as large as the Duke of York's country house where we filled the wagons with furniture, dishes and things made of silver.

I took one last look to see if we had left any valuables. I found a chest with silver spoons, knives, forks and candleholders and was pulling it across the floor so the boys could load it, when a floorboard popped up. Under the board I saw a metal box. When I opened it, I stood there and forgot to breathe.

I had learned my numbers when I was in prison, and I counted ninety gold pieces in the box. I put the coins in my leather pouch and replaced the board. Later I put my pouch in my bedroll.

We were all loaded and heading toward the warehouse that was half a day away. Our journey was almost over when out of the bushes several horsemen charged us. I slapped the lines on my team and put them in a dead run. They caught two of the drivers, but I was making it difficult for them by traveling through the brush. Out of the corner of my eye, I saw a horseman swing his cutlass. I dodged. He missed my body but I could feel blood gushing from my foot that was on the wagon brake. Then I heard a bugle and saw our Cavalry charge the loyalist robbers.

The Cavalry took my bedroll that held my pouch and me to our hospital. They bandaged my foot and gave me a bed for a few days. On the morning of the third day I was awakened by yells and gunfire. Drummers and buglers marched through our hospital tent. All the noise making was in celebration of the message that said the British had surrendered.

That afternoon a captain came to the hospital and announced that wagons were leaving soon that would transport injured soldiers home who were going south. I became one of ten passengers on one of the wagons.

During the three weeks it took us to reach the Alexander Plantation, I had the time to think and feel guilty for leaving my family. I swore to myself that I would make it up to them.

I felt nervous as the wagon came over the hill and I could see the plantation. Then I saw our house and my heart almost stopped. I got off the wagon with my bedroll that contained the pouch filled with gold pieces and began the struggle with my injured foot up the hill to my home.

I opened the door to go in and a big fat man I recognized as one of the prisoners in the Georgia prison rushed at me and shoved me back out the door so hard that it knocked the wind out of me. He yelled, "Don't you ever come around here again."

I thought I had lost my mind. There had be a reasonable answer to what had happened.

CHAPTER V

SOLDIERS ARE SELDOM APPRECIATED BY THOSE FOR WHOM THEY FOUGHT

ALEXANDER HAD PROMISED he would take care of my family so I headed for the big house to find out where my family was. But before I got to the house a couple young men accosted me. Was I ever happy to see Eric and Dobi. They grabbed me and sat me on a stump.

Of course I had to tell them what had happened to my foot before I could find out what had happened to the family.

Eric Told Me This Long Sad story.
It was in the fall after you left Papa. The harvest was great and we were all busy digging potatoes, gathering pecans and shucking corn. Then everything on the Alexander plantation stopped. Old Man Alexander died. The doctor said it must have been his heart that gave out.

We all gathered at the plantation cemetery and listened to the preacher. I was so tired from all the harvesting work, I went to sleep and didn't wake up until the preacher did his Amen's. They lowered William Alexander's body into the hole and threw dirt on him. I didn't realize how Alexander's death would change my life.

All the white families were invited to the big house where every table in the back yard was loaded with food. Dobi and I were always ready to eat so we got in line to have our plates filled. But the ladies told Dobi he couldn't get his plate filled there. He must go to the slave shed and get his food. I filled my plate and went down to the slave shed where Dobi and I cleaned our plates in silence. To this very day I am angry about what they did. I couldn't see why it would have hurt anything for them to fill Dobi's plate along with mine. I wish I could watch those old hags burn in Hell.

By December, Dobi and I had cut and stored enough fire wood in the cow shed to last a year, stacked enough hay to feed the oxen, the milk cow, the heifer and Tobins. For our family, there were crocks of dried fruits, vegetables and meat to last till spring. It was evening and a cold rain was falling but we were all snug as a bug in a rug sitting around the fire, eating popcorn.

Someone knocked on the door and Mama said, "Come in, if your nose is clean." Mama wouldn't have made that smart aleck remark if she'd known that the person who knocked on the door was Thaddeus, Old Man Alexander's only son. After his father died, he returned from France and swore that he would make the plantation a business that made a profit.

He stepped into the house, handed Mama a piece of paper and said, " I know you can't read so I'll tell you what the paper says: I, Thaddeus Alexander, the owner of the Alexander Estate, hereby notify Mary Carter who occupies ten acres of said estate, as a tenant, to quit and vacate said property within thirty days. He stepped up close and stared down at Mama. Mama was very short and Thaddeus was very tall. He pointed a finger into her face and said, "You and your family must leave this cabin and the field around it at once. Do you understand?"

"Mama told him that his father told Crinan, her husband, that he would take care of us until the war was over, if Crinan would join Colonial Army to fight the British. Where will we go and what will we do if we don't farm this place?

"Thaddeus shouted, "Mrs. Carter, the man who made those foolish promises is dead. I am the owner of this land and I say it will be used to raise cotton and the slave driver will live in this cabin. What you do after you leave this plantation is none of my concern." As he left, he slammed the door so hard the whole cabin shook. We couldn't understand why he was so angry unless he thought that if we hadn't taken advantage of his father he would have been richer. He didn't know that until we had made the hill a fit place to farm, the ten acres was worthless. We had built the cabin, the barns and the stone fence.

Dobi and I were so angry we were plotting the ways to kill Thaddeus. But Mama said she'd have no talk like that. 'Don't worry," She said, "We've got friends"

Our best friends live in the shed. The next morning we went to the slave shed and Mama told Sheli what Thaddeus said.

We knew the one person we could trust was Sheli. She was wisest person on the plantation. Old Alexander did too when he bought twenty-five year old Sheli from that Cherokee Chief. He had several tempting offers to sell her, but he would not. All the slaves went to her for advice and comfort so why shouldn't we?

Sheli said that, right from the beginning, when Thaddeus was a boy she knew he was no good. Spoiled so bad he only thought of himself and going to that school way over there across the ocean that didn't teach him anything that would make him a better person..

"Mama asked Sheli if she knew where they could go to get out of the cold rain? And what we could do when our food ran out? And when Crinan comes back, how will he find us?

Sheli told mama that if she were a slave, they'd take care of her 'cause she'd be property. They call you White Trash, she said and they don't want you nowhere around. But I know someone who'd let you stay with them, but it's a four-day walk from here.

Mama asked her how she could find them.

Dobi said that he knew how to get there because he had gone with his mother to visit the Chief when Alexander allowed them to visit some of Mama's friends.

Sheli told Mama that she would make a feather picture so Chief Concoch would know she had sent them and that they were her friends.

Mama's eyes got big, her mouth flew open and it looked like she was going to faint. Sheli put her arms around her and set her down and told her not to believe what "them snooty white folks say about them Indians. She said she belonged to the chief for eight years after she started bleeding and he let her be and made the young ones let her be but he sold her to Alexander and that bunch never let me be until I got old and wrinkled."

We all went to the Indians camp where Dobi and I have built a nice warm shelter and the ladies of the tribe and mama are good friends.

"But what did you do with the pigs, the milk cow and the heifer calves," I asked.

"We couldn't take the sow and piglets or the milk cow or her heifer calves and we could only take some of the hay. The Smithy bought everything else. Dobi and I delivered the hay on the sledge. Mama put the money in a belt she carried around her waist."'

"We filled the wagon with as much as we could stuff in and tied the sledge on behind with as much hay as we could put on it. Mama rode in the wagon, I drove the oxen and Dobi rode Tobins out in front cause he knew the way".

I was so angry I grabbed the musket Alexander had given me and started toward the big house. But for the boys, I might have gotten myself in trouble. There was one on each side of me holding my shoulders. Eric said, "Thaddeus is in Philadelphia doing some business about the people who will be ruling us now that the British don't rule us any more. We had a hard time but we're all right now and we are ready to go to the big river and get some land."

Dobi shook his head and said, "It wouldn't have been so bad but it was the time of year when there was cold rain every day. We were always cold and wet and Mama Mary got bad sick on the way."

" Yes," Eric said. "She slept on the bags of shelled corn but then we got stuck in a deep mud hole, even though she was sick she had to help. I was driving the oxen and Dobi was up front leading Tobins when we started across a low spot. The front wheels dropped in a hole and the oxen were stopped. I popped the oxen with a whip but I could see that no matter how they tried they couldn't pull the wagon out."

Mama said, " Unload some of the heavy stuff from the wagon."

" But it is raining and every thing will get wet." I said. "Maybe Tobins could help us. He is strong but we don't have a harness or a saddle for him, but maybe we can think something up."

I dug down in the wagon and found a cowhide and two sheepskins.

I tied the hide and the two sheepskins loosely around Tobin's neck and shoulders to protect him from the two thick hemp ropes I tied around his neck, like a horse collar. With one end of the ropes tied to the wagon tongue and the other around Tobin's neck he could help pull the wagon.

Although Mama was sick, she crawled down from the wagon to drive the Oxen. I took Tobin's lead and put tension on the rope. Dobi put his shoulder to the rear wheel. Mama shouted. Get Up! I touched a whip to Tobin's rear and he jumped. Dobi said he could feel the wheel moving a little.

"Mama said we must all pull at the same time, and that she would hold her hand up, and when she dropped her hand, she would put the whip to the oxen, I would put the whip to Tobin, and Dobi would put his shoulder to the rear wheel and push.

"We all got ready and Mama dropped her hand. The wagon began to move and as both the oxen and Tobins kept pulling and we started moving faster and faster until at last we reached solid ground.

"Mama crawled back into the wagon and we kept on going. That evening, we reached the Cherokee camp. When the women in the camp saw that Mama was sick, they carried her to their shelter, covered her with furs, put heated stones near her feet and gave her a kind of tea to cure her breathing sickness. The ladies wouldn't let Mama leave their shelters until she was well. She didn't get well until the dogwood bloomed.

I asked the boys why they were here if they were all right at the Cherokee camp.

Eric said, " We didn't know whether your army was winning or not or when you were coming back. Not knowing about the war was driving Mama crazy, she told us to ride Tobins back to the Alexander Plantation and ask Sheli what she had heard. Dobi and I rode double on Tobin's bareback. The Georgia spring was the best time of the year and we enjoyed riding, but most of the time, we walked. When we reached the ridge overlooking the Big House, we saw soldiers on the swamp road leading to the House. Some were walking, others were riding in wagons and a few rode horses. They didn't look as if they were attacking so we rode on toward the slave sheds.

"One of the wagons stopped and a soldier started hobbling on a crutch toward the cabin where we used to live. We couldn't see very well but we saw the soldier opened the door to go in but a big fellow pushed the soldier out the door so hard he fell on his back. He stood over the soldier pointing his finger toward the big house. On his way back into the cabin the big fellow picked up the crutch and threw it at the soldier. As we got closer we could see that it was you."

"Help me on Tobins" I said, "Watch that foot, it was half cut off with a saber. Bring the crutch."

There were things we needed to buy; a two wheeled cart, harness for Tobins and presents for Mary. I had the gold to buy them. We camped in the forest for a day while Dobi visited with Sheli who was so happy to see her baby who was taller than she was now. On the third day I hitched Tobins to the cart stacked high with supplies, tied my crutch on the side, crawled on top of the pile and said, "Let's go."

I pushed Tobins into a fast walk and sometimes a trot, forgetting that Dobi and Eric were walking. It took only two days to reach the Indian camp. Now the boys would need some new cowhide soles on their shoes.

It was near noon when we reached the camp but Mary wasn't there. I had a heavy feeling in my chest; I couldn't think. I looked around and sat down in this two-room shelter where a big cooking fire was blazing.

Dobi and Eric found Mama with a great load of firewood in her arms. As soon as she saw them, I heard her say, "How does Papa look?"

"How do you know we saw him," Eric asked.

" I knew he was on his way home even before I sent you, and I knew he was going to be here today. That's why I fixed the meat pies we're having for supper. I felt it in my heart and in my head."

When Mary walked threw the opening, I felt awkward. It wasn't like before, when I came home for a short while. Mary looked at the floor then at me. I was confused and I could see she was not sure what she should feel or how she should act.

Mary said, "How are you Crinan?"

I said, " It seems I've been traveling for years. My foot doesn't hurt any more unless I step on it wrong."

"How did you hurt it?" Mary asked

" I was riding in a wagon when a bunch of horseman charged us. All

I had was a pitchfork and they had sabers. Almost cut off my foot. I'll tell you about it later."

Mary walked over, took my hand, kissed it and rubbed her cheek with it. I didn't know what to say or what to do. All I could think of was that if I am injured, I can't do what she might expect me to do. All I could say was "I'm sorry I got hurt. I know I'm a cripple but I'll make it up to you."

After Supper, I took Mary's hand and pulled her aside and said, "Let's take my bedroll and go into the forest where we can be alone together. She smiled and nodded her head. I hitched Tobins to the two-wheeled cart, grabbed some skins, helped Mary on the cart and slapped the lines on Tobins. "We'll see you in the morning," I said.

That night we got reacquainted. We hadn't realized what time does to feelings between people. We thought things would not change, but they had. However, our love withstood the test of absence and our bonds became stronger than ever. Eventually I showed her my gold.

The next morning everyone was full of energy and resolve. We were going to the Mississippi River, get us some land and build us a home near it. It would be a place, where no one could throw us off because it would be ours. But first, we had to get supplies for such a long trip. We would need more tools and implements if we were going to farm and build houses. I had the gold to buy what we needed.

Mary stayed at the Indian camp while the boys and I hooked Tobins to the cart. We started toward the settlement they called Atlanta where we could buy a team of oxen, a wagon and implements to work a big farm. We would need another horse and harness in case we needed to work the horses.

After the two days it took to buy all the stuff, we headed back with the wagon loaded with tools and provisions we would need on our trip to the Mississippi. On our way back we took a small detour to the Alexander Plantation so Dobi could say goodbye to his mother. We decided to stay the night on some vacant land on the Alexander Plantation.

At first light the next morning I heard, " Get your self out of that bedroll and put on your boots." It was the Sheriff and Thaddeus. They were looking through the stuff in our wagon.

"This White Trash has no right to this stuff. The only way he could have gotten it was through dishonest means." Thaddeus said, " Both he and his wife were from the prison colony. They would not have been in prison had they not been dishonest thieves. My father was soft and let them live and farm a fine piece of land. Looks like they paid him back by stealing him blind."

I had experience with aristocrats in England. Thaddeus thought he was an aristocrat. But at least English aristocrats were honest. All the plantation owners thought they were aristocrats and were better than any one else because they belonged to the Anglican Church like the lords and ladies in England. They even tried to imitate their attitudes. They weren't the same but they made themselves believe it.

I knew better than to say anything against Thaddeus. He could have killed me and no sheriff would arrest him. I just answered the Sheriff as honestly as I could except that I told him that I had saved all my soldiers pay and used it to buy what I needed for my trip to the Mississippi. Still Thaddeus insisted that the Sheriff take me to jail. He told the Sheriff that he would keep the oxen and wagon at the plantation until he got back from Atlanta. Now as I look back this could have been a signal to me that such people as Thaddeus, although they were Americans would cause the people in the United States a great deal of grief in the future.

I was lucky that my remaining gold pieces were in the saddlebag on Tobins and that Eric had Tobins in the barn near the slave shed for Thaddeus would have taken the gold I had left.

That night the Sheriff took me to jail while Dobi and Eric were sleeping in the slave shed.

Sheli awakened them the next morning and explained as well as she could why the sheriff took Papa. She told them that Thaddeus was intending to take our oxen, wagon and everything in it after he got back from Atlanta.

Eric told me that Dobi looked at him, shook his head and remarked that he and Eric were not going to let "Mustard Face" steal our stuff. Dobi told Sheli to keep everyone away from the place where the wagon and oxen were. He said we were going to take our stuff to our camp. Sheli may have been proud of her son but I am sure she was afraid for him too

The boys gathered the oxen, yoked them to the wagon, tied the cart and the horses on to the wagon and started for our camp with the Indians. They heard that Thaddeus would be gone for five days so if Sheli could convince all the slaves to play blind and dumb, Dobi and Eric thought they could get to the Indian camp and back before Thaddeus got home.

Eric said his mama took the idea that I was in jail better than I thought she would. While Mary was fixing food and putting it in bags, the boys went to the wagon where the tools had been packed and got a file, a saw, an axe and a big rope. Sheli had told them that Thaddeus would not allow the law to release me for a long time. They would need the tools to break me out of jail.

They galloped Tobins and Smoky, our new horse, all the way back to the jail where I was feeling helpless. The boys stopped only long enough to rest and feed their horses. It took them less than a day.

Just before sundown, I saw them ride by the small one room jail, studying it very carefully. I hoped they wouldn't get in trouble trying to get me out of jail.

Eric held the horses out of sight in a grove while Dobi crawled under bushes to the window of the jail.

I heard " This Dobi here; this Dobi here; Mr Papa, we come to get you".

"Dobi, they better not catch you or they'll make you a slave again."

" We got a file, saw, axe and a big rope and we got Tobins and Smoky."

" Bring me the axe and hide in the grove so they don't see you."

A heavy cloud cut off the moon and starlight. I couldn't see more than ten feet away. I jumped when a cow mooed once. It sounded right close.

I started prying and splitting the wood around the iron bars as quietly as I could but sometimes it seemed so loud I held my breath. The cow mooed again and a calf answered. The cow and calf calling back and forth got louder and more often until it was a continual sound that almost blocked out the noise of breaking wood. A voice shouted, "Shut up". Then a door slammed and I could hear someone opening a gate. " Go to your mama but shut up," the voice said.

"Eric and Dobi where are you?" I whispered loudly.

I heard, "Over here,"

"Who's that out there? Are you trying to steal something? Come here and show ye self." A voice said.

I was crouched over with the axe in my hand when I reached our horses. "Let's get out of here," I whispered. Dobi held his hands together for me to put my good foot into, then I threw my bad foot over Tobins, kicked my heel against his sides, Dobi leaped on Smoky's back behind Eric. Eric whacked Smoky who would have left Dobi grabbing for air, if he hadn't been holding on to Eric's middle.

When I finally had a chance to look behind us, I saw a lantern moving toward the jail. We kicked our horses into a full out run and didn't slow down until the horses were lathered. As soon as we felt no one was behind us, we got off and walked to cool the horses.

When the sun rose, we stopped near a creek, loosened the cinches and staked out the horses to give them a chance to graze. We ate some corn bread and dried black berries. Dobi and Eric laid on the soft cool grass and went to sleep. In spite of my foot, I went to the top of the ridge and climbed a tree to see if we were being followed.

It was mid afternoon before I woke the boys. I told them several riders were tracking us and I thought they were four or five miles behind us, so we must get started. With rested horses, we moved rapidly and the next day we were among the Cherokees.

We told the chief and his council what had happened. They knew we were preparing to go the Mississippi but they suspected that the white riders would soon be there and cause them trouble. Yet, they promised to delay the white riders as long as they could. They told us they would try to trick them by telling them we had gone south to New Orleans.

CHAPTER VI
OUR JOURNEY TO THE MISSISSIPPI

EVEN THOUGH WE HAD ONLY ARRIVED at the Indian camp that morning, we were gone before midday meal. I felt like I was still in the Continental Army pushing a supply train, with an enemy on my tail. Oxen can travel seven or eight miles a day, but the horsemen following us could make twenty miles a day.

I had been away for so long I hadn't realized that Eric was now almost a grown man and could do a man's work. But my greatest surprise was to see how well he handled oxen. Mary told me that animals all seemed to like Eric and would do things for him they wouldn't for other people. "Maybe it's because he is so gentle and patient," she said.

Because Dobi was a good rider and seemed to have a feeling for the woods, I decided to have him ride out in front on Smoky and I would ride Tobin and bring up the rear. I needed to keep an eye on anyone who might be following. Eric drove the lead team of oxen and Mary followed behind with the other team.

After ten days without seeing the horsemen, we thought our Indian friends had sent them off on a wild turkey hunt. Better them hunting turkeys than us. The law had not gotten my musket as I had left it with Mary. I kept my musket handy in the back of the last wagon. We also had three bows and about thirty iron tipped arrows to defend our selves.

It was August and hot as blazes. We'd been traveling for about six weeks when I saw some riders a couple miles away. We guessed it was people like us going to the Mississippi to get some land.

It had been especially hot that day, so we stopped early. Mary was about to prepare some venison, but it smelled bad and had green mold on it. She shook her head, "We won't have any meat for supper tonight," and tossed the meat to the dog we called Cherokee because the Cherokees had given him to us.

"I'll go find some fresh meat, "Dobi said. He leaped on Smoky and headed off toward a nearby river.

Eric was in among a growth of willows trying to fashion himself a spear. He had found a broken knife blade and was tying it to a long straight willow shaft. Mary and I were sitting in the shade trying to cool off.

"All of you just stay where you are. Unless you want a ball through your gut," A voice behind me said.

Two men were pointing muskets at Mary and I. We started to stand. "Don't get up. Stay just like you are," the skinny one said.

The fat one went to his saddlebag and pulled out some raw hide and began tying our hands behind our backs and our feet together. "How about us having our way with this wench?" the fat one chortled.

The thin one said, "Lets get our business done first then we can think about pleasures. Thaddeus said we get no pay unless we bring back this fellow's head. You know Thaddeus means it. Hold his head down on that log and I'll cut it off with this axe."

I thought they were just going to rob us. If I'd known they were going to kill us, I would have fought them. Mary started screaming and crying. " I'll pay you gold pieces if you let us go," I said.

"We're going to take everything you got including the gold after we kill you. There is nothing you could give us to save your hide."

The fat one held my head on the log. I squirmed but he was holding me down with 200 pounds of fat. He kicked me in the head and dazed me. The skinny one raised the axe. I heard a horse's hooves pounding and out of the corner of my eye I saw a club strike the man holding the axe. I turned my head just in time to see Smoky turn around and start another run. The Fat one let go of me and grabbed up a musket and was taking aim. I could see better now and I saw Dobi making another run but I could see the Musket would cut him down before he got to the fat one. Mary could no longer make much noise and Dobi was about to be killed trying to save our lives. I was squirming like a snake trying to reach the Fat boy to bump him and spoil his aim. Then from out of nowhere I saw Eric with his newly made spear racing up behind the fat boy who was concentrating on his aim on Dobi. Eric plunged his spear through the fat and under the left shoulder blade. He dropped the musket but stood erect long enough for Dobi's club to practically take his head off.

Eric cut the raw hide that bound Mary and me. I felt the chest of the fat one. His heart had stopped beating. The other one was slobbering blood as he lay on his side but he wasn't breathing. I felt no heart beat.

Mary hadn't gotten up yet and Eric was stroking her hair. She seemed dazed.

Dobi got off Smoky with his club still in hand. He had tied a heavy stone on the end of a four foot long heavy oak branch. It was a mean looking weapon. We all stood there, not saying a word, just thinking. Eric went into the bushes and threw up.

"Are they dead?" Dobi asked.

"I couldn't feel a heart beating in either one"

Though Mary was still shaky, she was standing. "What'll we do with them," she murmured.

I remembered both these guys from prison in Georgia. I guessed Thaddeus had hired them to catch us. During the time we had been living on the Alexander Plantation, most of the ex-prisoners had eventually headed north into the hills of western Carolinas and Virginia but a few still hung around doing odd jobs and stealing for a living. These two probably didn't have any family so they probably wouldn't be missed by anyone except Thaddeus.

"Lets find some soft ground and put them in a grave," I said. "Dobi, see if you can find their horses and Eric and I will dig the graves. By the way, did you catch any thing to eat Dobi?"

" I got two rabbits," Dobi said, and handed them to Mary.

Dobi brought back three horses, two saddles and a pack mule with a quarter of a deer on it. We had also gained two muskets with a supply of balls and powder. All this was to our advantage, yet none of us felt well and no one ate much supper.

I didn't sleep that night. My mind revisited our experiences that afternoon and was riled about the danger we might be in if others were hunting us. I started planning what we'd do to protect ourselves. When we were traveling, I would hide in the front wagon with both muskets ready in case some one else wanted to rob us. And at night I would sleep in the wagon with the muskets. The muskets became my constant companions.

None of us slept that night. Dobi and Eric talked all night and Mary kept throwing her arms around me and sometimes I could hear a sob. We may have been tired the next morning but everyone was in a hurry to get going.

I hadn't counted on it being so far to the Mississippi. We had traveled for two months and the weather was getting cold at night. I didn't know how much further it was, and I knew if we didn't make camp before winter, we'd be in trouble. It would take a lot of time to gather grass hay to feed four oxen, five horses and a pack mule as well as build a winter shelter. If I took a couple horses and rode a day or two at a fast pace, I would know whether we could make it in a couple weeks. If it were too far for us to make it to the Mississippi, we'd have to make winter quarters and wait till spring to finish our trip.

That night I explained what I was going to do. Mary was a little scared about me being away for three or four days but the boys immediately started planning how they would defend our wagons if any more of theThaddeus louts were to attack us. Besides it had been six weeks since the attack on us. I didn't think anyone like them would want to be in the wilderness when the cold rain and snow started.

I would ride Smoky a few hours then I'D switch to Tobin and ride a few hours. That way I could ride at a trot or a gallop without tiring them.

It was the afternoon of the second day when I came over a low ridge and saw a giant treeless meadow more beautiful than Regents Park. It bordered a river so wide I had to believe that it was the Mississippi.

I rode for an hour before I reached the river. It was twice as wide as the Thames. Looking south down the river a boat was tied up to a wharf. Those people would know if this was the Mississippi. I had a couple hours before dark so I started south. But before I got to the boat, I came on several buildings where it looked like people were living.

I walked up to a cabin whose chimney was belching smoke and knocked on the door. A wild looking man whose small black, blood shot eyes stared at me as he opened his door and said something I couldn't understand.

"Is that river over there the Mississippi?"

"Yes, Mississippi" he said like a two year old child would say.

"Can boats travel all the way to the sea on it?"

He shook his head, threw up his hands and said "No Englais."

"Where did you come from?" I asked.

"Hispania" he said and slammed the door shut.

I would have liked to have learned about the country, but I would have to find out for myself, so I rode over to the wharf where the boat was tied. It was made of newly sawed wood and looked freshly built. They must have just made it. From that wharf I could send grain and cattle to a city they called New Orleans in exchange for gold. And we could buy things we'd need to have a fine house like the ones where Mary had worked as a chamber maid.

I kept up a fast pace on the way back as I was eager to tell Mary and the boys about what I had found During the three days I had been gone, they had moved the wagons twenty miles closer to the Mississippi. They weren't expecting me back so soon and when I rode through the trees near their camp, I saw a musket trained on me.

When they recognized me, they dropped their guard and raced out to greet me. I guess I could have waited till after supper to tell them all about what I had seen but I was too eager to wait. I had expected more questions but the only one I got was, "How long will it take to get there?" I hoped we would arrive soon enough to give us time to prepare for winter which I had been told was much worse than in Georgia.

It was a brisk fall day when we drove over that ridge and saw that wide meadow overlooking the Mississippi bordered by a thick forest. We stood there studying the features of this new land.

Dobi was the first to speak, "That's bigger Alexander's Place."

"We could put our house right there on that tableland next to the river,"

BILLY KRIEG

Mary said. "Could build a big house, but we'd have to have more children to fill it up."

Eric crawled on top of the wagon, in order to see another meadow in the forest. " I want to raise the fastest horses in the country right there in that clearing in the forest to the north." Of course, we couldn't see what he was seeing from his greater height in the wagon.

We built our camp on that flat table overlooking the river and began preparing for winter. Dobi found tall grass in the low spot near the river and began cutting it with the scythe, The livestock would require food when the snow covered the grass and when we were working them and they had no time to graze. Eric and Dobi took the axe and a cross cut saw into the woods and began falling trees and removing the limbs. Mary used a pair of oxen to drug the logs to the spot where I was prepared them to be raised into walls for our shelter. Each morning before the boys started their workday they lifted the logs into place and I would do the finishing work of fitting them together.

We had not yet put the roof on our shelter when the rains came. There was still much to be done. Though we were cold and wet all day we couldn't stop working and although we slept in the covered wagons, our blankets were often wet when we awakened in the morning..

One night as I lay staring at the canvas above me listening to the sound of raindrops, I was surprised by a sudden quietness. Quietness always make me suspicious but I was so comfortable I didn't want to get up and look.

The next morning when I opened the flap to crawl out of the wagon, I saw that the world had turned white with snow. No wild birds or animals moved. Quietly I waded to the covered fireplace that would serve as our fireplace in our new cabin and built a fire. But, we couldn't move into our cabin because we still had to stretch skins on the logs and branches that covered the roof.

I immediately started shoveling the snow that was in the space where we were building our shelter. As Mary, Eric and Tobi roused, they all saw what we had to do. Tobi grabbed a shovel and made the snow fly, Mary boiled up some mush that had strips of pork mixed in and Eric went to feed the animals.

By the end of the day, we had finished the roof and started moving

56

things from the wagons. Even though we got moved in, there was much to do to prepare for the unknown conditions of the winter we would be facing.

It was a long hard winter and a lot colder than Georgia. Most of those who lived around the docks had boarded the last boat south to New Orleans for the winter. Their shacks were bare.

When it was stormy we stayed inside and made harness, whittled wood into handles, yolks, plow handles and hitches. But on the good days, we were all out building fences around our land. We used stone and timbers and mounds. I figured that if we had a fence around the land and was either farming it or pasturing it, it would be ours. By spring, we had enclosed our three parcels with a fence.

Indians don't own land like us because they don't use it like we do. They were curious about why we were wasting our time building fences. Some of the young ones would tear down the fences just to see if we would repair them.

Dobi made himself an ugly mask and covered his shoulders with a skin covered with a white powder he made from pounded up rocks. He hid in the part of the stone fence. When some young Indian children started tearing down the fence, Dobi leaped out and screamed like a wild beast. The children ran and hid in the forest. Dobi jumped on Smoky and race into the forest screaming like a wild beast. The children never came near his fence again.

Each evening, when we returned, covered with mud, Mary would have clean clothes that were still warm from drying around the fire, ready for us before we ate supper.

CHAPTER VII
A NEW LIFE IN A LAND THAT REWARDS WORK AND PERSEVERANCE

AS SOON AS THE SOIL WAS DRY that spring we started plowing. Eric and I, each with a team of oxen and a plow, turned the soil in a way that the tough sod was turned under and the roots cut. Dobi, with four horses, drug a heavy log over the plowed ground until the clods of sod were broken and the seedbed was smooth.

The three of us worked together. For three days we planted my fields, then for three days we worked Eric's fields, and then three days on Dobi's fields. Then we would start the schedule all over again with three days in each of the three fields. After we had prepared the soil, we broadcast wheat and barley and drug a log over the field that stirred up the dirt enough to cover the seed. Then we made small furrows and dropped corn seeds at proper distances and covered them up. After the planting was done, tending it was up to the one who owned the land. But when harvest time came we planned to work together in the same way.

We picked a spot close to where we planned to build our house for a garden. We plowed it and leveled it. With forethought Mary had collected all her seeds in the fall before she was forced to leave the plantation. During the days just before she had to leave the plantation, she dug up bushes, young fruit trees and cuttings. Now was the time to start preparing for our food for next year. With artistic glee, Mary worked all day planting and designing her orchard and garden like she was painting a picture.

That was the most beautiful spring I had ever experienced. Everywhere plants grew and flowers bloomed and the boats started going up and down the river. People began moving into the vacant shacks on the river. Everywhere there was activity and energy. I was surprised by the number of families who came on boats from the north looking for land to settle. Some brought cattle, pigs, and fowl. We were happy to see them whoever they were. They were someone to talk to and trade with. There was no one who held themselves above anyone else. We traded the packhorse and a gold piece for two heifer calves and a bull calf, which was the start of our cow herd.

That summer, since the boys were staying with us, they helped build more of our house.

They had no need for a house without a family. It was a good learning experience since they would be building their own houses soon. Before the rains started we had built three more rooms that we covered with wood shingles we made from trees we had cut the winter before to make our first shelter.

Mary was with child again. We figured the baby would be coming some time in October. So about two weeks before she was due to birth, we put her in our two-wheel cart and took her to Mrs. Cordova's house. Mrs. Cordova had been an aide to a doctor in Spain and was an experienced midwife. She and her husband, a Spaniard from New Orleans, had come that spring to start a mercantile business. They were both educated people who spoke English very well.

After Mrs. Cordova examined Mary, she warned that Mary would need help and that she would need it as soon as she started having the birthing pain. I agreed that Mary should stay with the Cordova family until the baby was born.

I'll never forget that date. It was February 14 when she was born. It wasn't a boy but for some reason, as soon as I saw her, I loved her and in my mind she was the most beautiful person I had ever seen. It did not take long to figure that she was smart. It was hard to imagine that she was the daughter of such a stupid old man. We named her Ester. I called her Ester with the golden hair.

Ernesto and Marta Cordova became our special friends. When we had a surplus, we shared it with them.

One of the people who came during the summer after Ester was born was a shipwright who was also a preacher sponsored by a Protestant group who wanted him to teach the Indians about their God. We heard that his wife and daughter were good at reading and writing.

We were landowners and now had built two more rooms in our house that made it a five room house. Mary and I thought it seemed fitting that Eric and Dobi learn how to read and write. In my experience, I had seen that in a civilized country, reading and writing was necessary. Furthermore, Mary and I could not read or write but if our children could read and write, they could do the reading and writing for us. I watched over Ester while Mary, Eric and Dobi went to see the preacher's wife about teaching the two boys to read, write and cipher. I didn't go cause I never wanted any truck with those crazy preachers. She would teach Eric, but she said that she couldn't teach a Negro how to read and write. To me that showed me I was right about their stupidity.

Dobi was just as smart as Eric and could learn just as well. Eric was angry about this. "Everything I learn, I'll teach it to Dobi.," he said. You want to learn to read and write too, don't you Dobi?"

"I want to read the Bible to my mama. She'd be right proud of me."

Over the next year Eric and Dobi learned more and more words and how to cipher. They spent hours yelling and giggling and learning. If you learn at the same time you teach what you learn, you learn faster and better. Soon they were reading every piece of print they could find. They wrote each other letters and messages. They even wrote signs that included printing on a board they nailed to a post outside. They said the words printed on the board said, "This is the house of Mary and Crinan Carter."

When people noticed that Dobi was reading print on products, they were amazed for they had been told that Negroes were not smart enough to read. Some were disturbed, for they said that if slaves learned to read they would revolt.

The reading and writing brought a change in Eric's and Dobi's lives. But although it broadened how they looked at things, their lives still required much hard labor. Those who owned the amount of property that my sons and I owned in England would have poor people to do the hard labor. Similar landowners in Georgia had slaves to do their hard labor.

One of our hard labor jobs was harvesting grain, for that was the only thing we could raise that we could sell for cash.

We cut our grain with a scythe that had a cradle attached. As we swung the scythe in a semi-circle motion starting on the right and passing around in front in a single swath, the heads all fell backwards and the stems were driven forward. At the end of the swing, the partially green stems and heads fell into a wooden cradle attached to the backside of the blade that kept the heads in one direction and all the stems in the opposite direction. Before starting a new swing the grain was dumped in an orderly bundle. Later we gathered several bundles and put them together standing them on their stems with the heads loosely facing the sun to dry. These large multi-bundles of wheat, oats or barley are called shocks. In the fall we went to each of the shocks with a grain box on a wagon. We threw the shocks into the box and flayed the grain from the straw. Then we pitched the straw out of the wagon box. When our wagon box was about half full, we hauled it to our granary for storage.

In the spring, our animals worked hard but in the fall the humans worked harder. Swinging the heavy scythe and cradle, or gathering the bundles into shocks or flaying the grain or shoveling the grain into storage all day was hard work.

Those four summers after we got to the Mississippi River went by so fast it's hard to remember all the work and planning that went into that time. All three of our farms had fences around them and our house was taking form. We had a parlor, a big kitchen, a pantry and an upstairs with bedrooms but it wasn't the same as we knew in England. It was still crude because we couldn't buy the fine things to make it like we wanted for we didn't have money. Even if we did, there was no place to buy what we needed. We had all the grain we harvested last year and would have more grain this year. Even though, there were many people settling around the wharf, we could sell only a small amount of what we grew and therefore we had no money.

After Eric learned to read, he liked it so much he was always borrowing books. Dobi could read but he was best at ciphering. Didn't even have to have a paper and pencil.

There was no telling how much these boys could learn from all that writing. I had always thought that you had to be wellborn and rich to be able to learn reading and writing. But those boys showed me that anyone could learn even if they were black. I wished I'd had a chance to learn to read and write.

Eric and Dobi were hanging around the mercantile store listening to the stories of the river boatmen. They came to realize the possibilities of selling everything they grew in New Orleans for very high prices. They were so excited they rode at a gallop all the way to where I was yoking the oxen. " We got a way to get silver and gold," Eric said.

I finished hooking the harrow to the team and said, " Speak your mind boy."

"Dobi and I want to go down river to the city of New Orleans and make a covenant with a shipper to exchange our corn, wheat and cattle for Napoleon gold pieces. If we get gold we can buy some modern tools fine things for our women folk."

I knew about covenants from listening to merchants in London. To me, it was a handshake promise written down on paper, but I didn't know how they worked. If those boys could do what they said, I was for it. "How many days will it take?" I asked.

"The boat takes about ten days, " Dobi said. "The boat master said he'd take us down and bring us back, if we'd help unload his boat when we got there."

I knew them boys would be having a big adventure and when they got back they'd have some tales to tell. It could be dangerous but if they didn't try some things that were dangerous they'd never learn anything. I gave each one a gold piece for expenses.

A week later, Mary and I went to the wharf to see them off. The boat they rode was about fifty feet long and about twenty feet wide. They called it a keelboat. There was a little shack up front where they put some food and their bedroll. They would be sick of cured pork, sauerkraut and dried fruit before they finished the trip.

Almost six weeks later, Mary and I were sitting in our kitchen after supper when the back door opened with a smash. Both of us were startled and jumped up.

There they were no worse for the wear. Two young men, who started talking at the same time as they walked in.

Eric said, "We were curious about how that boat worked, so Kessler, the captain, let us help him run his boat.

"Yeah! Captain Kessler said doing it is the best way to learn," Dobi added.

Dobi continued, "We didn't use the sail. We just used the poles to stay in the current. The boat was loaded with pigs and corn. Our job was not only helping with the poles, but we fed the pigs."

They were on the boat for about ten days when they saw some tall buildings down the river. Captain Kessler told them that it was New Orleans. But it took them almost two days to reach the buildings. It took them fourteen days, not the ten days they had expected. While tied up at the dock, rain was falling but they had to unload because the wagons were waiting to pick up their loads.

The hogs didn't like the rain any more than the boys did. One old sow broke loose and the boys chased her into the yard surrounding a very large home. The sow smuggled her way into the carriage shed out of the rain. Inside the carriage house they tried to corner the sow so they could fall on her and put a loop of a small rope around one of the front legs. They thought they had her cornered and leaped on her but she was a big one. She jammed her nose between their legs and took off with both of them on her back carrying them straight into some hanging harness that fell on them and entangled the sow and the two of them into a web of leather. Then the side door of the carriage house opened and a tall young slave girl stepped through the door.

" What's all this fuss going on out here?" she yelled. They told her they were trying to catch that sow.

When she saw their predicament, she began to laugh so hard she bent over and held her stomach.

"It looks like you caught her", she said, "Now what are you going to do?"

The sow freed herself and headed toward the door where the girl stood. She forced the sow back into the carriage house, grabbed a rope and shook out a small noose. She threw it at the pig's feet, expertly drawing it up quickly around one foot. She had caught the sow while we were still struggling to free our selves from the harness.

Dobi said, "That girl had a sassy mouth."

She told us that when the two of us got loose, she expected us to hang up that harness and straighten it out like we found it. She said she would hold our sow while we are doing it. We put everything back like we found it and thanked her.

Eric asked her if there something they could do that would repay her for helping catch the sow? She replied, "Well, yes, I guess if you come back after a while, I'll have something you can help me with."

Dobi and Eric took the sow back through the rain and finished unloading the boat. Dobi said he wanted to be alone with that girl so he and Eric decided that Eric would find a place for them to stay the night while Dobi helped the girl. Later Eric picked him up at the girl's place.

I knew those boys would have an interesting time, but I wanted to know if they had found someone who would buy our grain?

Eric explained, that while he was waiting for Dobi, the boat captain told us of a Spanish Sea Captain who bought enough grain to take several shiploads a year. He sold it in Europe. The next day we went to see him and told him that the three farms could give him 900 bushels of corn and 800 bushels of wheat. He agreed to pay us one Spanish gold dollar for each bushel of corn and two for the wheat. He put on paper what he would pay us in three parts depending on how much each of us sold to him. We carried the contract to the United States office where we signed our names. I signed for you, Papa.

When they went back to the keelboat for the ride home, the Captain said he wouldn't be able to return for a couple months. Dobi and Eric both said they knew it would be a long walk home.

Dobi wanted to walk fast because he wanted to get home so he could spend more time on building his house. He suddenly realized that he had been neglecting it. They said they thought they walked at least twenty miles a day. The land was level and there was a wagon road all the way. It had taken them a little longer than three weeks to get home.

That night I couldn't sleep for thinking. I knew about merchants in England. If it was not to their advantage to honor a handshake agreement and if there was no way to make them honor the agreement, they would not. We had pieces of paper with marks on them that would burn if you touched a flame to it. We had to sell our grain if we wanted to be paid for all our efforts. But I must not spoil the optimism of my boys. Optimism is what makes living worthwhile. Then I asked myself, why did Dobi want to spend time alone with that slave girl? I had never thought about Dobi having a family. Tomorrow, Mary and I would talk it over as we always did about making important decisions.

CHAPTER VIII

ERIC BECOMES AN ADULT
SOONER THAN WE THOUGHT. .

ERIC GOT MORE FROM HIS VISITS to preacher Harvey's house than just how to read and write. I understood that every time he went there, their daughter, Emma, greeted him at the door and saw him out when he left. One time she even visited us with the excuse that she had to deliver some reading papers to Eric.

I thought she was a very beautiful girl and when I talked to her, I was even more impressed. She was a couple years younger than Eric and the two of them were just about the same height and looked similar, except that Emma had brown eyes and hair.

That summer both Eric and Dobi started working on their houses. They had dug wells earlier to water their livestock. By late summer both had built two rooms and a privy and had moved in. But fall came, and we had to start spending all our time harvesting the grain. Still Eric found the time to visit the Harvey house. He said he still had a lot of learning yet to do.

It was evening, and there was no light in Eric's house. We were watching for him when we saw him walking his horse slowly toward our house. We went out to meet him to find out where he had been. He would have ridden right by us if Mary hadn't yelled out, " Where have you been? Is anything wrong?"

He seemed to awaken from a stupor and rode over to where we stood.

"Where you been?' We were getting worried about where you were. The Indians sometimes kidnap lone riders and sell them for slaves to those western savages."

"I was at the Harvey's house talking to Emma. Then we went for a walk through the trees by the river."

It struck me that wasting time walking in the woods was very unlike Eric. "Do you like Emma?" I asked.

" Sure, she is a nice girl."

"Does she like you?"

"She kissed me on the cheek."

"What did you do?"

"I kissed her on the mouth."

"Did you like it?"

He looked down to the ground and mumbled, "Yeah."

I decided I had questioned him enough so I changed the subject by telling him that we should be able to take our grain to New Orleans soon.

It was less than a week later when Eric asked me how he should ask Emma to marry him. I didn't want to admit I didn't know. I did know what I had heard about the way respectable people did it. So I told him that.

I had been able to get acquainted with Mr. Harvey and found that he was a regular man. Not snooty like those preachers in England. Once when we were talking about building a boat for the Mary and I, he told me what happened when Eric asked for his daughter's hand

He said, "On one of the days just after Eric had completed his lesson, he was sitting with us around the fire. He seemed to be nervous about something. Then, as if the impulse just suddenly struck him, he went directly to where Mrs. Harvey and I were seated. He went down on his knees and with his head bowed blurted out: 'If Emma and I were to get married, would it be alright with you?'

"I feigned ignorance of what I well knew. I looked at Nora and Emma and acted very perplexed. Then I told him that I didn't know that he and Emma were courting, but that our family would have a discussion. I went on to tell him if he would come back Wednesday, we would give him the answer.

" He started out the door, but then turned around and said, 'You know I have a large piece of land and I am building a house. I have three rooms built already.

"He abruptly turned around and started for the door, then just as abruptly turned back. He went to Mrs. Harvey, took her hand and gently kissed it. He did the same to Emma's. Then with head bent he grasped my hand and gave it a gentle shake. He backed out the back door and just as he left he shouted, 'I'll be back Wednesday.'

"I believe it was probably the next morning after the day he had asked the Harvey's for Emma's hand, that he showed up as we were eating breakfast. He looked as if he hadn't slept that night. It seemed that he had raced from optimism and dreaming to pessimistic despair.

"He said, 'I am only five feet two inches tall. My hair is red red and my eyes are so pale blue that you can hardly tell the whites from the blue. Why would Emma want to marry me or' why would any girl marry me? I guess I'll just stay a bachelor all my life. But Emma has already told me she loved me. I would make her proud of me. I will build her a house she will be proud of, and we can have lots of children and grandchildren.

"Because Eric was so fond of fast horses, I thought if I gave him Gates, it would give him the self confidence he needed with his love life. Gates was the fastest horse I had ever come in contact with. I would not have owned him had not his owner, a recent emigrant from Ireland, fallen on hard times. I called the horse Gates because that was the name of a politician who thought he was a general. When the redcoats made its first push against his army, he was so frightened that he turned tail and ran his horse over a hundred miles to his home and never again tried his hand in military or political matters.

Early Wednesday morning, Eric mounted Gates and ran him all the way to the Harvey house.

Eric told me he knocked on the door and Mr. Harvey invited him in where he joined them drinking tea and answering questions. Emma wasn't there as she had gone on an errand to a neighbor's house. Finally, Emma burst into the room all flush and pretty. She had seen Eric come and she had run all the way home. Emma put up her hand and said, "Just a minute

Eric Carter. Before I make my decision whether to marry you or not, I want some answers to some questions."

As I understand it, these were the questions and answers.

'Do you love me? '

'Yes, with all my heart.'

'Will you love me forever?'

'Yes.'

'Will you love me even when I am cross or when I get old and ugly?'

'Yes'

'Alright, I will marry you but are there any questions you want to ask me.'

'No'

When Eric broke the news to Mary and me, he also told us that Mr. Harvey had invited Mary and I to supper next Monday night to make the wedding plans. Mary threw up her hands and exclaimed, 'Oh my,' and sat down with her hands on her head. 'What will we do?'

I said, 'We'll have supper with Mr. and Mrs. Harvey and Emma and plan our son's wedding so we can start having grandchildren.'

Mary was a nervous wreck during the days before the supper with the Harvey family. She sewed, polished and washed every day. She talked about the weddings she had helped her mistress prepare years ago. She told me that certain people would make cruel gossip about those people who didn't do everything just right. She even got me to oil the harness and clean the cart.

Although, I did not like preachers because I could see they defrauded people who couldn't read by telling stories that gave the preachers power over honest people. Preacher Harvey never mentioned those marks on paper that these people used to cheat innocent people. Mary need not have worried for Mrs. Harvey had no idea about a proper wedding except for what her husband said was proper.

When we insisted that Dobi would be the best man, The Harvey family was shocked, but when we told them about Dobi's bravery in saving our lives twice, and that he could read and write and cipher and when we said he was a freed slave and a land owner, Mr. Harvey agreed that such an unusual Negro deserved recognition.

The way Harvey talked about the average Negro as if they were some kind of cattle to be used as objects did not set well with me. On the way home, I told Mary that I thought those preacher people were hypocrites, always talking of love and kindness until it actually came time to be loving and kind. It seemed they always had excuses that didn't make sense. Even so I told Mary that for Eric's sake I would think of the preacher and his family as regular people.

Eric told me that he agreed to be baptized as that would make Emma happy.

He told me that the river water was warm and it felt good to be dunked. When his Father-in-law finished the baptism, Eric asked if that was all? He had expected it to take all day as it had in the Cherokee ceremony.

When Emma and Eric stood on the wharf and listened to Mr. Harvey say those magic words about them agreeing to love each other forever, Eric said he thought of Mary and me.

CHAPTER IX
THE WAY DOBI STARTED A FAMILY

IT WAS NOW THE EIGHTH SPRING and summer that we had been on the banks of the Mississippi. We now had a place to sell our grain and a place to buy products from the world. Furthermore, we had enough experience with the land and the weather to get the most from it.

During that spring and summer everyone worked. The dishes and clothes were dirty because the women were working in the field. Ester played at the end of the fields and even Emma, a preacher's daughter, joined the work force and felt good about what she was doing.

A hailstorm beat some of the plants into the ground and rain came when we were trying to harvest the wheat. But we did thrash 5oo bushels of wheat and after we had shelled the corn, we calculated we had 1500 bushels. We would once again be able to meet the terms of our contract. It was then that I began worrying about whether the Spanish Sea Captain would and could buy our grain for the price that we had agreed on. From my early life, I had seen how those who had money, education or the upper hand would take advantage and cheat the poor and ignorant. But we were not poor anymore we had property and grain, furthermore, we could always sell the grain to someone else. And two of us could read and write. That would help defend us from the cheats. I didn't feel sad or fearful, but I did feel anxious.

We loaded our wheat and corn on a keelboat. Eric and Dobi and I boarded the boat and set off for New Orleans. Captain Martinez had built a warehouse in New Orleans where he had an agent who paid us in Spanish gold after we unloaded our grain. The agent made us another contract, but this time we agreed to sell him twice as much grain. We would have to plow up some more land but that would be easy. "If we don't grow enough", Dobi said, "we can buy from all the folks living up north at a cheaper price and make a profit."

In New Orleans, we divided the money we were paid for the grain according to what we had contributed. Dobi handed back some gold pieces and asked, "Will you buy a girl for me?" I was taken aback. I didn't know Dobi knew about things like that. He must have learned a lot on his first trip.

"Dobi, I don't know where to buy a girl."

"I want to buy Sahara, she belongs to Mr. Dubeau. They live over by that wharf"

"Why do you want to buy Sahara?"

"I love Sahara and she loves me. Eric met her and he knows she is a fine girl."

Now, I understood. "If he will sell her, we'll buy her."

We were lucky. Mr. Dubeau needed the money more than he needed another mouth to feed. Sahara was about the same age as Dobi and she was beautiful. Now I understood why Dobi wanted her. After the Bill of Sale was signed we started back to the area with the shops. Eric wanted to buy some presents for Emma and I wanted to buy some things for Mary and Ester.

Sahara and Dobi walked behind holding hands and talking up a storm. They had serious feelings about each other and how they wanted to spend their lives together.

"Mr. Papa, Sahara and me want to marry," Dobi said. " She knows a preacher. We'll be back at the wharf before sundown."

I remembered Mary and me that afternoon in Georgia. "That's a good thing to do' I said.

"My first name is Dobi. Can my second name be Carter?"

This boy who had saved my family once and my life once was a worthy person to carry the Carter name, no matter that he was a tan color. "Your names will be Dobi and Sahara Carter.

Had we been able to take our horses on the boat we wouldn't have to walk back and carry all the things we had bought. In our hurry to buy for those we loved, we failed to have taken this into account. How was Eric going to carry a French style drawing table and how was I going to carry two rocking chairs. How would Dobi and Sahara carry their bedstead?

When Sahara saw all we had planned to carry over the great distance to Chickasaw Bluffs (That's what they called Memphis Town in those days), she made a suggestion in her cute French accent, ' Wagons go to north to buy many things to put on the ships.' Maybe for gold pieces some will haul us and all this stuff to Chickasaw Bluffs."

We all thought this was a great idea but how do we find these wagons?

Sahara said, " I show you."

She and Tobi went together and were gone for at least an hour. Finally we saw them with two wagons following them.

Sahara told us that she would have to talk for us since we did not speak French. She began negotiating as soon as the lead driver reached us. After some time and after a lot of gesturing, Sahara turned to us and announced, " For twelve franks or six Spanish dollars they will haul all of us and our stuff, but we have to feed ourselves and provide our own bedrolls."

In our purchases, our eyes had been bigger than our stomachs and we were delighted at this turn of events. We all knew who to thank and quickly divvied up our equal share of the money.

The three girls we left at home had spent most of the time we had been gone visiting each other and when the wagon train pulled into our yard, they were having lunch. They were a little frightened at all those loaded wagons coming up the lane to our house until they saw us. They rushed out to see us and were delighted when I introduced Dobi and Sahara Carter.

It was something new for Sahara to be treated as an equal among white people. But she followed Dobi's lead and soon became a little more comfortable.

For the next few years our three families were prosperous. Emma and Eric started their family with Martha and Kenneth. Dobi and Sahara had a son they called Maurice. Every year was better than the one before. New settlers moved in around us. Three more wharfs were built and hundreds of houses crowded around them. The settlement even had a bank and a lawyer. We had heard that we were going to be a state of the United States, and it was going to be called Franklin. Later that year we were told that come the first of the year, all the land here was now a real state just like Georgia. Congress had made it a state in 1796. It had taken a spell to get things organized, and our state was Tennessee instead of Franklin.

The settlement down by the wharf was called Chickasaw Bluffs, because every year the Chickasaw Indians camped there in the winter.

Ester had grown up more beautiful than any girl in the community and with the help of the parson and his wife she became educated and accomplished, especially at the piano and on the organ. Eric helped me place an order for a piano in France. I used the last of my gold pieces from my time in the war to help me pay for it.

The piano was delivered to the wharf. But we kept it there for about a month and had it tuned before we brought it home on Ester's seventeenth birthday.

Although Ester was seventeen years old she had never had a serious beau. I thought she was going to be a spinster. When we invited people to her birthday party we only sent invitations to the people in the Church where Harvey was the preacher and Ester played the organ. But we were not aware of some of her other acquaintances who were very well educated. Joan, a girl friend she had met when she was learning with the Preacher Harvey's wife, asked us if we had invited certain friends she and Ester had in common. Emma and I were surprised. This was a part of her life we had not shared.

This was not our first surprise for at the party she paired off with a certain young man who had been introduced to us as George Madison. We had heard of his family who had come to the Bluffs from Baltimore.

They were in the shipping and trading business and were very wealthy. They built a great house and a complex of buildings on the river. Their only son who had been educated in Virginia had reached the ripe old age of twenty-one without ever having a serious female friend, until he met Ester playing the organ at a wedding of his friend. One look and they knew. Just like Mary and me.

The piano was the perfect gift for Ester. She played it at her party to the appreciation of her audience who insisted on many encores. The party represented a change in Ester's life.

Within a month, she and George had set their wedding date. Although we met George at Ester's party, we really didn't get to know him because he was so quiet and very matter of fact, no foolishness. He was all business even the courting was like a business.

We were invited to the Madison home to meet George's parents and discuss the wedding they had planned for their son. It was not like we did with Parson Harvey which was a cooperative affair. This wedding was what their son was having. Ester's roll was to fill in as the bride.

We saw no need to disagree and besides they would be furnishing everything. We were sure that life after the wedding for this couple would live up to their lavish wedding.

We enjoyed the wedding and met many important people who all commented on our daughter's beauty. We felt that Ester would have a good life and prove to be a compliment to both the Carter and the Madison families.

With a fine home, fine horses and with all our children able to read and write, we felt very respectable. Just when things are at their best, there's always something' to mess up the contents of a good life and that something was a lawyer, a banker and a sheriff that rode a buggy out from Memphis Town

They handed us a piece of paper and Eric read it. It said that a man know as Thaddeus Alexander owned our farms. He owned all three of our houses, our barns and anything attached to the land.

CHAPTER X

IN A SITUATION THAT YOU
DON'T UNDERSTAND, YOU
HAVE TO TRUST SOMEONE

PARSON HARVEY WAS AN EDUCATED MAN and honest for a religious fellow. We carried the paper over to his house and asked him what it meant. He said we needed to talk to the lawyer who had bought the mercantile store from our Spanish friends.

Mr. Hazard, the lawyer, explained that just because we had cleared the land and built fences and buildings on the land, it didn't mean that we owned it. Some time ago, this land was Georgia Territory. Thaddeus Alexander with the aid of a few dollars given to the poverty stricken members of the Georgia legislature convinced the government of Georgia to deed a large chunk of the land on the Mississippi to him. Much of the land has become part of the new state of Tennessee who legally had to honor Mr. Alexander's deeds. He said our homes belonged to Mr. Alexander.

But, the banker had not come along with the Sheriff for nothing. After the Sheriff gave us the news, the banker told us that he was authorized to sell our homes as one farm to us at a reasonable price.

The next morning the three of us went to the bank and told Edward Jackson, the banker, that we wanted to buy our homes. He didn't answer right off. He just sat there making marks on some paper. "I can get you clear title for the whole piece of land and the buildings on them for twenty thousand dollars." He said it in a way that sounded like he was giving us charity.

We didn't have more than three hundred dollars in Spanish Gold among us. We looked at each other and started to leave. Jackson held up his hand and said, "I know you folks have worked hard improving that land. I'll sell it to you but you must pay me a little each year until you have paid $60,000.

"How much each year?" I asked.

Jackson wrote down some ciphers and said, "Each year for twenty years, you will deliver a payment of three thousand dollars to this bank no later than the fifth day of January each year."

I was getting older and I was in no shape to pick up and go west to the Territory across the Mississippi and besides, with the money we'd been earning, we could have paid much more. It's best we get this thing all legal so we wouldn't ever have to worry. " Write all that down like you said. Eric, Dobi and Mr. Hazard will read it so we know what we handshake to do," I said. " But, if I do what I promise, you had better do as you promise, or you and Thaddeus will go to Hell before your time." Jackson acted like he didn't hear. Probably had been threatened before. But I meant it.

Eric and Dobi signed their names and I made my mark. Our three places were one held in a partnership as Crinan Carter, Dobi Carter, and Eric Carter. Mr. Hazard had made the Partnership with the marks on the paper.

Mary and I wanted all our homes paid for so that all our children, and children for generations to come would never have to work for someone else. I knew that if they worked at the bidding of others, they would work without passion, their work would be hateful and they would die without ever having lived. No Carter should ever have to hold a job. It is like being an indentured servant.

Most years we grew enough wheat and corn to meet our contract with Captain Martinez who gave us Spanish gold. We used part of it to pay the bank. But in 1809 Martinez sold his warehouse and stopped buying. We started selling to the American who bought the warehouse. He always tried to pay us with paper money from some bank. I didn't take to that and insisted on gold. I knew how bankers played with paper money cause they were the ones who printed it That was why they called them bank notes. Not one of them had ever put in a good days work; They lived by cheating. We didn't put our gold in the bank. We kept it in an iron box with stones cemented around it. Each one of us kept our gold in a little box in our big box.

Making payments of three thousand dollars each year had seemed like an easy thing to do, but it was much harder to do than we thought. After New Orleans became an American city and there were so many others growing grain. If the weather and the insects allowed us to have a good crop, the buyers in New Orleans would hardly give us enough to pay for our seed. If the weather was bad or we had smut in the corn and wheat, and we wouldn't have enough grain to bother about taking to New Orleans they would offer a good price. More than once Dobi, Eric and I had to take money from our savings box to make the payment. Eric didn't often have much in his savings, maybe because he had so many children.

By 1825, we would have paid what we owed. Then we all would use our money to build granaries and store the grain when we had a good crop and not let the middlemen's greed buy our grain for less than it cost us to raise. We wouldn't sell to them until a bad crop brought a shortage then they would have to pay us a decent price. Until we had paid the bank, we would just have to tighten our belts cause we had to sell our grain to pay the bank

Eric and Emma started their family right off. Martha was born ten months after their marriage and became our first grandchild. She began walking and talking at nine months. She didn't get to be the baby of the family very long for Kenneth, her little brother, was born a year later. Martha became the big sister and was given responsibilities beyond her years. Perhaps, that is why she matured so quickly.

But three years later, another brother Roy, was born. Now, Martha, who was only five years old was expected to help with two siblings. Then before we knew it, Sahara had her first child and now we had four grand children. One evening, Dobi came to visit. He had a problem that he needed help with. He wanted to communicate with his mother Sheli. She couldn't read and knowing the human quality of her owner, it was clear he would not take the trouble to deliver a letter and read it to her.

I suggested that if he wrote the letter that Eric and I would see that it was a part of a letter we would have delivered to the Smithy. He would send a message to Sheli to come to his shop and he would read the letter to her. A few days later Dobi gave us several pieces of paper covered with writing. On some of them he had drawn pictures very accurately of his house, his son and Sahara. Eric took Dobi's letter in an envelope and placed it in a package with his letter asking the Smithy to send the message to Sheli. He took it to the new office in the town that sent letters to the office in the town of Athens where the Smithy lived.

Chapter XI

Things Happen That You Don't Understand But Only Savages Blame It On Their Gods

It was in the middle of winter and my roof was leaking. I gathered up some pinesap and began heating it. I made some shingles. Then I leaned the ladder up to the roof of the porch and started up the ladder. For no obvious reason the ladder began to slide back and forth. It jumped up and down and began to slide off the roof with me half way up the ladder. When I was younger I would have leaped off the ladder and landed on my feet. But I went down with the ladder and twisted my arm.

Everything kept on rolling and shaking. I was wondering if I was ill, for I felt as if I was on a ship in a rolling sea. Suddenly everything became quiet.

I stood up and went in the house. Mary was setting in her rocking chair holding her head.

"What's the matter," I asked.

"I am dizzy. I think I am sick. Everything is swaying like the ship that brought us to Georgia."

"I felt the same. I couldn't keep my balance on the ladder and fell off. I think I broke my arm."

No sooner had I gotten the words out of my mouth then things started shaking again. It wasn't rolling like before, but shaking. The dishes in the cabinet were shaking and the front window shattered. Then we heard the bending and breaking of timbers and the crash of the roof on to the second floor.

After the shaking stopped, I grabbed Mary's arm and two comforters. We went down the hill to the meadow. We sat on a log with the comforter over our shoulders and talked about what we had just experienced. My arm hurt, but what had just happened was more important and we needed to understand it.

I told Mary that we had to accept the fact that we were getting old and that we could no longer do everything we could when we were younger. We knew that often old people become dizzy and sometimes after these spells they became paralyzed. For most of our lives we had felt together, thought together and worked together. Maybe now that we were old people we would also have those old people's problems together.

But my mind told me that was not probably what had happened. Things don't happen that way. I had seen landslides, and I had watched great waves wash upon the shore. Many things made of dirt, rocks and water do unusual things and can be understood by examining and investigating real material. I may not have understood this. The older I got, the more my experiences taught me that I just had to look more closely at what was happening. Each season as we grew crops, we learned something new. That is why our ground grew more grain than any other farmer on the Mississippi.

Mary thought it would be interesting to see if the shaking and rocking of the earth did something to the river. So we hitched up the buggy and headed to the river.

As we neared the river we heard some shouting and people speaking Indian words. We tied the horse to a tree and crept through the forest. The Indians were holding a religious ceremony. Perhaps they believed that their Gods were unhappy with them. We went back to the buggy and headed to the river a different way so as to avoid the Indian ceremony.

The river had over flown its banks and was a mile wider. Maybe a thunderstorm happened and so much water came down the river that the weight caused the land near the shores to sway and shake. We were still very curious and wanted to know more. Perhaps the people in Memphis town, who were more educated than Mary and I, could enlighten us. So we headed into Memphis Town to see if they had experienced the same shaking and swaying as we had. As we neared town, we felt the swaying and I had a difficult time controlling Dolly our old mare. It only lasted about a minute.

We saw no one until we reached the town square. It was crowed with people and a traveling preacher was yelling at them, saying that because the people in this town were sinners God had shaken the earth warning them that if they did not change their ways they would burn in hell. He had his book on a table that told him that the end of the world was near at hand and that what we had just experienced was just the beginning of the end. Every so often he would hit the book with his hand as he explained how the world would be destroyed by fire and that sinners and nonbelievers would burn forever, however, the believers and the virtuous would go to heaven and live forever.

As we sat and watched, Dolly cocked her ears as she listened to the noise. Two or three ladies were passing among the crowd with plates and bowls collecting money for the preacher.

Two men passed close enough to hear us ask them if they had felt the rolling and shaking of the earth. Yes, they had felt it.

I ask them if they knew what caused it.

They both said, "God."

I ask them how they knew.

One said, "What else could it be"

The other said, "It says so in the Bible.'

"Have you read where it says that in those Bible papers"

" No, I can't read."

I looked up. The scene had changed. A long line of people were lining up and walking passed a low table where they knelt down and the preacher threw some water on them and mumbled some words I couldn't understand.

Mary looked at me and said, " You know I remember what some people told me when I was a cleaning maid. If I asked why, they always said, (Because I said so.)

We decided to visit Eric and Dobi. They could read books about things that other people knew. Some people in England and Scotland had a way of thinking about natural things that made sense. Maybe the boys can find some books that would explain why the land makes the rolling and shaking motion.

Dobi, Sahara and their family were visiting with Eric and Emma when we got to Eric's house. After the greetings from all ten people, I said, "What do you suppose caused the swaying and shaking motions." Dobi looked at Eric and Eric smiled as he said, "Oh, you mean the earthquake."

It was then that I realized that our family had raised itself from the bottom of the servant class to a position in which anything was possible.

Dobi said, " Most people think the land is solid but it is not. The land we think is solid sits on a bunch of rocks that are piled on top of each other with dry dirt holding them together. If rain, wind or something affects the rocks and changes their balance, the whole thing begins to move and shake until it reaches equilibrium. We think that is what happened. " There are records where it happened in Italy and other places and in other places in the world."

I heard him say we. That led me to believe that they had been talking about what had happened. Their explanation about what had happened made a lot more sense than what all those other people thought.

We heard from people who lived far up stream where the shaking had been much worse. The water from the river had spilled over into some of the flat lands along the river. We were fortunate since none of our three farms were touched although our land reaches the riverbank in several places.

Two months later we had another earthquake. The ground swayed and shook. After it was over I visited with some towns people at the mercantile. They still insisted that the latest shaking was just a second warning to the sinners. I did not contradict them, as I knew they would never change their mind and it might cause hard feelings if I disagreed with them. I know that some people get an idea in their heads and if the facts don't agree with their idea, they will re-shape the facts so it fits their idea.

CHAPTER XII
MEN CHEAT, STEAL, DEFRAUD, AND ENSLAVE OTHERS BUT THE WORST OF ALL CRIMES IS WAR

MARY AND I WERE BUSY DIGGING in the dirt when Martha rode up on her horse. She didn't see us so she called out, "Grand Papa, Grand Mama, some travelers just told us that the British just burned down the house where President Madison lives and are going to take over our country.

I had heard that the British were blockading our coast so we couldn't trade with any other country. The grain buyers had said that they couldn't buy any grain until the blockade was lifted. I supposed that we were using our Navy and Army to fight them off.

In Tennessee, we were having our own problems with the Indians. I do not know but I suspect that the reason we had several Indian uprising in 1813-14 is because we had so many white people, who like Thaddeus, were arrogant, dishonest and insulting. The Indians thought of themselves as people who were just as good as any other people. When such people as Thaddeus mistreated them, they would fight back

I had known war and didn't like it. When there came a call for volunteers for the militia to fight the Indians, many young boys and some older single men gathered and under the tutelage of Revolutionary War veterans such as me. Although I had never actually fought with the Army, I had proven myself to be a good scout. I taught the tactics of a scout.

I was very happy that I had convinced Eric and Dobi that war was one of the worst insanities of man and that being a professional soldier was not only a stupid occupation, but was dishonorable as well.

The soldiers we trained had five engagements during 1813-14. They accomplished nothing and showed themselves to have a disposition to panic and run. We had taught them how to fight, but we could not give them courage.

In Nashville, Tennessee, a man named Andrew Jackson was put in charge of the Tennessee Militia. Jackson had 2500 militia and a band of Choctaw and Lower Creek Indians who were mercenaries. He soon got them in shape even though he had to execute a few who panicked and ran.

By the end of 1815, not only had Jackson defeated all the warring tribes but had also defeated the English in New Orleans. The country had been at war with the British for three years. .

During those three years, we shipped grain in all directions, some went down to New Orleans and some north up the Ohio River. We got double the price per bushel that we had gotten in the years before the war. It was lucky for me because age had reduced my strength and stamina. With the extra money I could afford to hire help to take my place in the field.

I guess in all wars there are winners and losers. I can imagine that the ship builders and makers of guns and powder in Britain jumped for joy every time their country went to war. If they could urge the nation into war either with money or propaganda, they did it.

I asked myself if I should feel guilty because we had made more money during the years we were fighting the British than we had before. I couldn't answer myself.

Chapter XII

Some Things You Just Don't Expect

I HAD SEEN THE LORDS AND LADIES of England file into large halls where famous people performed. Attendance at these affairs indicated that such people were superior creatures to those who didn't. Yet, I had seen rats and spiders attending these affairs.

Ester had given us a special invitation to her performance in the opera, Don Giovanni. This was the first musical to be performed in the new assembly hall. The director and some of musicians were from London. They may not have been the best from London but they were the best in the U.S.

Because Ester was a performer, Mary and I sat in front seats as honored guests to watch the performance. As we waited for the music to begin, I reached over and took Mary's hand and squeezed it.

The new Mayor of Memphis walked to the center of the stage platform. The Governor of Tennessee followed and was introduced to the audience. The Governor said," Will Crinan and Mary Carter stand up please?"

We stood up.

" Will you come on stage please?"

I followed Mary as she climbed the steps on to the stage and stood before the Governor.

He spoke his words in a slow loud voice. " As a representative of the Citizens of Tennessee I wish to honor two people who have help build or state into one of the major state in this country. From a wild and primitive land they have created some of the most productive farm land on the Mississippi River. They built three of the finest homes in Memphis. They have raised and educated a family that would be a credit to any community. To show them our appreciation for their efforts, this community awards this special good citizen plaque to Crinan and Mary Carter.

He handed me the plaque and the crowd clapped all the time we were walking back to our seat. The music was some of the best we had ever heard and Ester was better than ever but we couldn't understand the words in the songs very well. As we rode our surrey home that night we talked a lot. I said, "Can you imagine what certain people in England would think if they could see us now?"

Mary squeezed my hand and said, "What would Thaddeus Alexander think?"

The Queen of England may have a higher position but she was born in that position. She did nothing to do reaching this position. She had nothing to do but entertain herself. What would be the point of building something or becoming better when you had gone as far as you could go?

Mary and I thought of ourselves as builders and farmers and an important part of the land where we lived. There were many who had far more wealth, but who have not participated in creating either their wealth or the building of their country. They are lost in an empty space.

Perhaps we were feeling just too proud of ourselves for the next morning when Mary was driving to join Emma in a quilting party her buggy horses were frightened by those young Indian boys who enjoyed causing trouble. The horses bolted and threw Mary out of the buggy and on to sharp bush that resulted in a gash in her right leg just below the knee. She called it a scratch.

A few days later Mary stayed in bed cause she was hot with fever. I threw back the blanket and saw a swollen leg that looked like so much rotten meat. Then I began to cry, for I had seen men with such wounds in the war. They usually didn't last through the night.

I told Eric to get doctor Lewis and to run that dam buggy horse all the way. He left out of there at full speed and came back just as fast but without the doctor. He burst through the door and began explaining, "Mrs. Lewis said the Doctor was away for a spell but just as soon as he returned she would send him, she gave me some alcohol to bath the wound and told me how to get the swelling out. She said to take young chickens and while they are still alive cut them open and wrap them around the wound and leave it their until the blood started clotting. Then get another one and do the same.' She said to do the same with the next chicken and keep doing that until the doctor got there."

I told Eric to get a chicken while I bathed her leg with the alcohol

Eric started bringing chickens, and I started opening them and wrapping them around Mary's leg. Soon there was a pile of dead chickens outside the door.

The doctor arrived a couple hours later and rushed in to find a frenzy of activity and Mary crying with pain. He cleaned off the wound with alcohol, shook his head and said, "That leg is going to have to come off."

Mary didn't hear what he said but I did. I pulled the doctor over and whispered, " Wouldn't that be too painful for her ?"

The doctor said," Get her some whisky."

Eric heard and was out the door in a flash.

The doctor was busy preparing Mary for the operation while I comforted her. I rubbed her hair and washed her face with a warm rag and explained that no matter how bad the whisky tasted she must drank all she could because it would stop the pain while the doctor was operating on the sore. I didn't tell her that the doctor intended removing her leg at the knee.

Eric returned with the whisky and Mary started drinking. She had never tasted an alcohol drank and made a terrible face and almost vomited. The more she drank the easier it was to drink more. When everything was ready the doctor tied Mary down and ask Eric and I to make sure that she did not move the lower part of her body.

By the time the Doctor was ready to begin, Mary had passed out. It was all so painful to me, I closed my eyes and held my breath as long as I could. Eric just set his jaw and looked away.

Dobi and Sahara arrived about five and a short while later Emma and

Martha joined the family in the parlor. Preacher Harvey and his wife arrived a few minutes later. Followed by several other neighbors.

I told Preacher Harvey that if he thought prayer would help Mary, he could lead us all in a prayer. He gathered everyone in a circle, knelt down and started saying prayers. I couldn't understand what he was saying, but if it would do any good, I was for it. I was so helpless and I felt so guilty because I hadn't protected Mary, and now I couldn't help her.

Emma and Sahara prepared and served a late supper for everyone. But Mary was sleeping soundly and seemed out of danger. Eventually, everyone except the doctor finally went home. The doctor laid down in the guest bedroom, and I laid down beside Mary but I couldn't sleep.

Over and over my mind retraced our lives together and what it meant in the great scheme of things. If I had not met Mary what would have happened to me. Would I have just continued my life like a wild beast in the wilderness, living by my wits and cunning without the enjoying the more human experiences of empathy and love? And what would have happened to Mary? She had been made helpless, then turned out, like a domestic animal, to suffer as a victim of the harder, soulless elements of humans.

If we two people, the most pathetic, could bring forth the feelings we had for each other, why can't everyone? Perhaps it was the space in America and the freedom to express all those things in us that helps us work together to build and grow. The freedom from those who tell you how to live, love and build allowed Americans to become the best they could. These things in America would make a nation that would become greater than all others. In this terrible time of pain and sadness I had found something positive. My children, grandchildren and great grandchildren will live where it is possible to experience the joys of expressing all the human positive feelings. No one will force them to do what someone tells them is good for them by promising rewards of heaven or the threats of pain, for their own logical mind will make it obvious to them what is good and what is bad. I could tell them all about this, but they might just call it the ravings of an old mind. Even if they did understand it, they would probably forget it. It would probably never pass on to more than one generation.

If I could have written down like the people who wrote the Bible, it could become a permanent record and each Carter generation could read it and learn. And if each generation contributed their story and added it to the book, our descendents would have the benefit of many minds. In this way, we could help the young people in the future recognize that the history of their country was not limited to politicians and generals, but included ordinary people who did the work and were responsible for innovation, creativity and productivity of their country.

Mary made a noise that aroused me. I put my arm around her and whispered, " I am here and you are going to be all right." She threw her arm around me and exhaled. We stayed in that position until the dawn awakened me.

Mary's arm was stiff and when I looked at her face her eyes were open and staring. I rushed to where the doctor slept and pulled him into our bedroom to look at Mary. He probably knew Mary was not alive but he went through the motions and pronounced her dead. I asked the doctor to do what was proper, and I went to the barn and cried.

Eric and Dobi and their families made all arrangements. A special place was walled off in our yard where our family members would be buried.

Preacher Harvey asked me if he could deliver Mary's eulogy at graveside. I said, "What is an eulogy?."

" It is a speech given to all the people who have come to the grave side to pay their respects. It is about the life of the person who has just died and something about what kind of a person she was."

"How would you know what kind of person she was and the story of her life?"

"You and your children would tell me."

" It would take you all day to tell the story of her life and another half day to tell what kind of person she was."

" Only tell me some important things about her and her life that you would like the community to know."

I told him all the good experiences we had and left out the bad things and I explained that her love had made me a better man and our children better adults. The preacher wrote all that down and said it just before we buried Mary. The newspaper took a copy of it and printed it the weekly paper.

Sahara, Doby and Ester prepared the food that fed all those who attended the funeral. I got into my buggy and drove to the river. I didn't want any one to see what was happening to my mind. It was private between Mary and me.

After everyone had gone I went to the grave side and set for several hours. I began preparing my mind for my death

The next morning I went to see my solicitor, Ezra Hazard. I gave him my instructions for the distribution of my property. Ester was very wealthy but would have first choice of whatever furniture or mementos she wanted. Dobi would have my land that joined his down by the river and Eric would have the rest. They each would have an equal amount of land so they could earn enough to pay their share of the mortgage.

Then I explained that I would dictate the life story of Mary and me. Upon my death, copy of this story must be given to each of our three children. There were also instructions at the end that explained why they must add their life story to ours and pass it on to their children. This I explained was the beginning of a dynasty and a piece of the history of their country.

It took a week for Ezra Hazard's secretary to write the story.

As Crinan Carter's solicitor, I have followed his instructions and six months after he dictated this story I presented copies to each of Crinan and Mary Carter's three children.

The Parson Harvey asked that the following copy of the eulogy he had delivered at Crinan's funeral to be added to the Carter Story

" I wish to describe the life of Crinan Carter, a man whose stature may have been small but who had a giant spirit. He came into the world without a father and when he was five years old, he lost his mother. He never had a friend or a relative to teach him the things adults teach young people until he met Mary, who not only became his wife but became both a physical and a spiritual partner, inseparable like the two sides of a coin.

Yet, this man raised a family and built one of the finest farms in Tennessee. And because he appreciated the freedom in the colonies, he was willing to help our nation free itself from Britain by fighting in the Revolutionary War.

Although Crinan was not a Christian, he lived a life that followed the ethics of the Sermon on the Mound. I would like to believe that had he been able to read the Good Book, he might have become a Christian.

He leaves a daughter, Ester and two sons, Eric and Dobi.. He said that this family was the beginning of the Carter Dynasty.

The family buried Papa beside Mary in the front yard of their home where Dobi carved the words, " A man that all young men should emulate."

PART II
Moving on in America

The Story of the Second Generation of the Carter Dynasty

1818 to 1843

CHAPTER I
EMMA CARTER CONTINUES
THE CARTER STORY

I AM EMMA CARTER the wife of Eric Carter. I held Eric's parents in high esteem. It is for this reason that I have taken on the responsibility of writing the story of our generation in the Carter Dynasty. I am sure that if Eric's mind was still sound, he would already have added to the Carter story. Please excuse me for having the audacity to write this story for the Carters.

The Mary and Crinan partnership had a single direction, which was to be free to become the best they could. Crinan always said that it was not enough to be free from kings or governments, but to be free from men who because of their weakness, find it necessary to lie, cheat and steal the products from the labor of others and who betray and use others for personal gain.

I watched them toil in tranquil bliss with a joy far greater than I ever saw in the idle, whether rich or poor.

I was raised by a man of God who professed to live a life his according to the Bible. At first, I was shocked when I heard talk so disrespectful about Jesus and God. If the conversation tended toward religion or politics, Crinan would find some chore to do. Both of them called it "Jawing Nonsense." I soon learned that they lived a very ethical life with moral standards higher than my own father's.

I met Eric when he began coming to our house to take lessons in reading and writing taught by my mother. He was shorter than me, but I thought he was cute with his straw colored hair. Eric endeared himself to my parents with his sincerity, honesty and gentleness, and when he asked for my hand in marriage, my parents were delighted.

Crinan and Mary thought there was nothing wrong with getting married in a church if it made their marriage more legal. After all, they had used a man of God to make their marriage legal. When Eric insisted that Dobi be his best man, there were murmurs in the settlement and my parents were very uncomfortable. Dobi was tall with light colored skin and fine features. He carried himself proudly and looked so regal. I had no objections. It did not prevent people from coming to our wedding. We had over forty people at our little church; most of the men had to stand up. Everyone was always looking for an excuse to get together, and if they didn't have to travel more than a day's ride, they would be there. The wedding was an all day thing. We had the ceremony at nine in the morning and spent the rest of the day socializing. We had horse races, horseshoe games and lifting contests. Mary and my mother spent all day cooking and serving, and by sundown, everyone was so tired and stuffed with food that they went to their camps and within an hour everything was quiet.

Eric and I started our family right away. Martha, our first child, was a year old when Dobi returned with his wife. Kenneth was born three years later and in two and a half years, Roy was born.

Two years passed before Dobi and Sahara had a child, but over the next three years they had three more children.

Eric acted as if he had been waiting all his life for Martha, our first child. He began taking her with him to do chores when she was two years old. Sometimes she rode on the front of the saddle or perched on his shoulders. When Eric did things like feeding the animals or hauling things, Eric gave her little chores to do, like bringing a bucket that was often as big as she was. She felt proud because Eric always complimented her. The older she got the more responsibility Eric gave her. By the time she was ten, Martha was responsible for feeding the pigs and chickens, bringing in the cows from the pasture and milking them.

It was the morning of October 15 on Martha's tenth birthday. Eric had left at the crack of dawn to meet with grain farmers up the river. He expected to be back before sundown to celebrate her birthday at Crinan and Mary's house. I had been complaining about not feeling very well. Mary suggested that I send the two younger boys over to her house that morning. Martha hitched up Old Bird, our buggy horse, and I put Kenneth and Roy in the buggy, Martha slapped the lines and headed down the road a mile to Mary's place. I was glad to get them out of my hair for the day. I was expecting our fourth child in about a month and felt uncomfortable and cross.

First, the pain came to my back, then the pain in my lower stomach bent me over and I went down to the floor. Martha had come back to do her chores and was feeding the flock of chickens when she heard me scream in pain. She rushed in just in time to see me picking myself off the floor. "What's wrong," she said.

" I have a pain in my stomach and I need Doctor Best to come fast." Ten years old was much to young to understand what was really wrong with me. I had given birth to three children but this was different. It was much too early and the sharp pains were different than before. I was frightened for I had known so many women who died while giving birth. I grabbed Martha's arm and said, " Get Doctor Best for me as fast as you can. Listen carefully and tell him exactly what I going to tell you. 'Mother is very sick in the stomach. She is losing blood and she says it is over a month till her time. She wants you to come at once.'"

Martha unhitched the buggy from the horse, led him to a rail fence, scrambled up on the top rail of the fence and then crawled on to his back. She had brought a willow switch with her, and with that she put Old Bird into full run. With a hand full of mane she kept him at top speed until she reached doctor Best's house three miles away. She slid off old Bird who was wringing wet with sweat and tied him to the fence.

Doctor Best heard a child's voice and a banging on the door. The doctor's wife went to the door where Martha recited what she had been saying over and over while riding bareback at full speed. "Come in child," she said, "I'll get the doctor."

Martha told the doctor she was Martha Carter, then repeated what she had told the doctor's wife. " Kathryn, I'll be out to Eric Carter's place.

Can't say when I'll be back," the Doctor said in a voice Martha told me later sounded real serious.

The Doctor grabbed his bag and mumbled as he began throwing other things in the bag. He didn't harness his buggy horse but threw a saddle on him, cinched it up, stepped into the saddle and headed for the Carter's at a fast gallop.

Although the doctor's wife wanted her to stay a bit for some milk and cookies, she would have none of that. Martha remembered that her father had always told her that after you have worked a horse till he is in a lather, you best walk him till he cools out. She knew that there was something terribly wrong with her mother, and she wanted to get back. She started toward home leading Old Bird at a fast walk.

I had looked at the clock when Martha left. It said 8:30. I was frightened and in pain but I hadn't expected the doctor to arrive in forty- five minutes. Dr. Best said later that had he arrived thirty minutes later, I might have bled to death. When Martha arrived home, the doctor met her at the door and told her that her mother would be all right and that she should rode to her grandmother Mary's house and ask her to come over as soon as possible.

That evening Martha celebrated her eleventh birthday with Crinan, Mary, Kenneth, Roy, Dobi, Sahara, and their children. Eric brought Martha her birthday gift late in the evening. It was a filly fourteen hands in height and shiny black. When Eric told her she also had a little sister whose name would be Rosemary, Martha broke down and cried. The excitement of the day had been too much. Eric picked her up and cuddled her. A few minutes later she was back to her old self again and wanted to go out to the barn again to see her horse. That night a few seconds after she pulled the quilt to her neck, she fell asleep. This was a birthday she would never forget and the older she got the more often she told the story of her eleventh birthday.

CHAPTER II
ERIC'S CHILDREN

MARTHA RODE HER BLACK FILLY she called Angel to school and as soon as Kenneth got old enough to go to school, the rode double on Angel. Since Dobi's children were not allowed to go to school, Sahara brought them to our house where Martha became a teacher for not only Dobi's children but for Roy and Rosemary. They all learned to read simple stories at five and could write their name.

Eric had always wanted to have the finest horses in the country but he never had time to train them. Besides, he wasn't strict enough, and the horses knew he was a pushover. However, he had a son who was a superb horseman. Kenneth was taller then Eric by the time he was thirteen and rode a horse with a posture you would think he was an aristocrat. With superb patience he would let the horse take his time to think about what was expected of him. Eric bought the horses and judged their breeding but it was Kenneth who trained them so well that when Kenneth rode them in the ring at the Memphis auction, the bidding got hot. Kenneth's reputation as a horseman spread and he was paid by a very wealthy landowner named Finn to train and show his horses.

Martha and Orville Roarck had been friends since she was ten and he was fourteen. The Roarcks had come from Maryland and bought land in Tennessee just after it became a state. They had done well and had five boys and four girls. Orville was the youngest.

Orville borrowed a down payment from his father and bought one hundred sixty acres from the banker. Two years later, even though he had a big mortgage he asked Martha to marry him. The engagement was to last for about six months or until he got their cabin built.

After Martha's marriage, Crinan and Mary looked forward to their first great grand child, but they were never to see Betsy who was born three months after Crinan died.

After Mary and Crinan died, we could have moved into their house as it would have been more comfortable, but we didn't feel right about moving in. The memory was too fresh. Eric said that from the time he was a youth, almost every night, he heard his mama and papa talking and planning. Their planning would last longer than he was able to stay awake. However; he was always frustrated, because even though he put his ear to the door their voices were so quiet he couldn't understand what they were saying. Now when he was in their house, he still heard their voices coming from the bedroom.

Eric thought that if he re-modeled the house, his parents' voices would go away. "I'm going to make this house the finest in Tennessee," he said. "Mama and Papa always talked about the country houses of the lords in Britain. I'm going to make this house, right here in Tennessee, as great as any lord's. I'll put a bronze plaque on the front gate that will dedicate the house to Mary and Crinan Carter.

CHAPTER III
BEING RICH MAKES UP
FOR BEING SHORT

DURING THE NEXT TWO YEARS, Eric could talk of nothing else but the house. He spent a lot of money and even hired men to help with the spring planting so he could work on the house. By the second summer, we moved into the largest and finest house in the county with a third floor and big white columns that held up the front porch roof. Father said it looked just like the plantation homes in Virginia where he was raised.

Next to the settlement, we had called Chickasaw Bluffs a lot of rich men began building businesses and houses. They didn't like the name that reminded them of Indian savages so they changed the name to Memphis after the famous city in Egypt. These new people weren't as friendly as those who had lived in the Chickasaw Bluffs. They thought they were better because they had more money.

We were getting just like them, thinking we were special because our parlor had expensive glass and silver chandeliers that showed we had class and money. Eric convinced my father to solemnize my sister, Alice's marriage to Daniel Roark in our parlor. The wedding was the most grandiose social event that had ever been held in West Tennessee. Everybody who was somebody came dressed in clothes they thought would have been worn by the aristocracy. Their buggies were polished and their horses curried. The wedding was not like ours. It had a lot of flash, but it lost the feeling of two people and their tender feelings for each other.

With such a fine house, Eric was driven to build new barns and fences to match. His corn rows had to be as straight as arrows. Everything on the place had to be perfect, even though he had to borrow from the banker to pay for it.

Although we were the same people, the behavior of our neighbors toward us became more respectful and less friendly because of our house. I missed the friendly attitude of our friends and felt guilty, but Eric acted as if he deserved it and became a community leader. Some times I felt embarrassed. I began to see a side of Eric I either refused to see or I had just been blind to it. Eric, who was only five foot tall seemed to be insulted by the height of those who were taller than he. He vacillated between timidity and arrogance. Like Andrew Jackson, his hero, Eric insisted that in all things he was absolutely right and that to disagree with him was an assault on his person.

At a meeting of Shelby county officials, a newcomer from Pennsylvania was heard to say, "Jackson's backwoods behavior is unbecoming a President and he has disgraced the U.S."

It was as if the man had struck Eric in the face. Eric shouted, "You are unpatriotic and I insist that you recant that statement."

The fellow, named Canfield, shouted back that he had a right to express his opinion as this was a free country, and that if Eric wanted to do anything about it, he could come outside and they would settle the matter right now. Eric said that the man had a right to free speech but not the right to lie and slander the greatest president the States had ever had. Eric slapped Canfield's face and challenged him to a duel. Canfield looked down his nose at Eric and said, "Bare fists, day after tomorrow at sunrise in the Shelby Courthouse Square."

Canfield was almost a foot taller with long arms. I was not so much worried about Eric being beaten as I was of what Eric would do if he got beat. Would he be so embarrassed that he would do something crazy that would hurt the family? I knew I was powerless and my suggestions would be looked upon as an example of a woman's lack of understanding men.

The whole countryside had heard of the coming battle. Several Jackson

Democrats visited Eric out in the barn where they advised him on ways to defeat the Whig lover. Eric was sure of his victory, but I wasn't so sure. Of course I didn't let on to Eric that I didn't have the confidence he did.

I really didn't want to go but I thought it was best if I was there to bind up his wounds and make him feel better for having lost. A mile before we got there, we could see the oil lanterns and hear the people. The streets were already crowded by the time we got there. The people who had voted for Jackson came to cheer Eric and the Whigs came to see Eric get thumped. There were three times as many Democrats as Whigs. This match was going to divide this county more than it already was.

An area was already roped off to separate the audience from the fighters. The county officials sat on a platform next to the fighting area. They were talking to Canfield when Eric and I made our way through the crowd. Eric had some leather bands that he intended wrapping around his knuckles. He said it was to keep him from cutting his hands on Canfield's sharp nose. He crawled through the ropes and showed his leather wraps to the officials and to Canfield, and Canfield showed Eric his deer skin wrappings.

Roy had gone into town a couple hours before we left. He hadn't said why,. but it soon became clear. He had a fire going under a pot of boiling water where he had added tea leaves. Behind him was a sign tied to a tree. It said, " one cup of tea, six cents." About ten people were standing around his fire drinking tea. When they handed back the cups, Roy would wash them out at once, dry them on a cloth before filling them up for the next customers. Why Roy loved to make money, I didn't know, for he never spent any of it.

As the rays of the morning sun struck the Mercantile store, the county official stepped out of the roped off space and said, " You may fight."

The two fighters moved to the center of the ring where Canfield took a swing at Eric's head. Eric dodged. The momentum of the swing that missed threw Canfield off balance enough to give Eric time to run in and punch Canfield in the stomach with such a heavy blow it seemed to double Canfield up. Eric ran in again to strike another blow, but Canfield had recovered enough to meet Eric's charge with a blow that staggered Eric. Canfield, seeing his advantage, rushed in to finish his opponent. He drew his arm back so as together as much power as possible. He intended this to be his one and final blow necessary to finish off this undersized jackal. He swung the blow, beginning at his ankles, putting all his weight and strength behind it. He missed again, but this time he lost his balance and had to put out both hands on the floor to keep from falling on his face. Canfield's head was now low enough for Eric to reach. Eric leaped on that head and poured blows on it. Canfield dropped to the ground where he lay unconscious. The crowd roared. Eric stepped out of the roped off area and bowed to the crowd, took my arm and said, "Lets go." W e crawled into the buggy and started home. I looked back and saw two Whigs helping Canfield out of the rope enclosure.

After we had gone about a half- mile, Eric said, " Take the lines while I remove the leather bindings." As he unwrapped the leather, he uncovered a small cylinder of lead from each hand that he had gripped to make his fists harder and heavier. I could now see why Eric's blows were so telling. He looked at me, smiled and said, " These were to make up the difference in our size."

With his victory, Eric became the leader of a group of local farmers who rode to the Hermitage where they talked to Jackson and stayed all night. Eric returned with his chest stuck out. He imagined himself an unselfish man with a fatherly concern for his flock whose mission was to restore equilibrium and moral balance in his community.

I noticed that Dobi and family his had stopped visiting us since Eric had gotten on his high horse. Dobi had been Eric's best friend but I don't think Dobi and his family ever crossed Eric's mind except when Dobi took our farm products to New Orleans and contributed to his share of the bank payments.

CHAPTER IV

THE HIGHER YOU GET THE FURTHER YOU HAVE TO FALL

ANYONE WHO HAS EVER FARMED for very long knows, no matter what is done, things can go wrong. You can't do anything about the weather, or the people who control prices for products that you paid for with sweat and sacrifice.

Starting in 1829, we had several years of bad weather and low prices, but we managed and paid our mortgage payments. However; in 1836 things turned around. The weather was good and we sold everything we raised for the highest prices we had ever received. Eric was so proud when he deposited his bank notes in the Memphis bank.

While Eric was at the bank, the banker, Mr. Bain, gave him a notice that said he had sold our mortgages to a lawyer in Memphis named Ralph Finn.

Eric knew how a person could sell wheat or a horse but how could you sell a handshake debt. Mr. Bain said that Finn bought the Carter's handshake promise from him and now instead of paying Bain's bank, he must pay Mr. Finn the same amount on the same date. However, after three more payments they will have paid off the mortgage and would own their land with a legal title. Although he didn't completely understand, he didn't make a fuss.

I remember that fall day in 1836 when things started going wrong like it was yesterday. Eric went to the mercantile store to buy some leather to fix the harness. He handed George his bank notes to pay for his purchase. George said, "Those banknotes aren't worth the paper they're printed on."

Eric read the printing on the notes, "The bank of Memphis guarantees that the holder of this note may exchange it for an equal in silver from the Bank of Memphis."

George said "Go to the bank and get your silver, I'll take it in payment for the leather."

The Bank was closed and it was closed the next day when Eric tried to get his bank notes exchanged for silver. Eric went to Mr Bain's house to get the silver for the bank note he promised. His house was bare and someone had broken the windows.

Eric soon learned that the bank had become bankrupt and everyone who had kept money there had lost it. It was as if Bains had stolen everyone's money and gotten away with it because he was a banker.

Eric must have been too ashamed to tell Dobi or me but when the time came to make our payments, Eric went to Ralph Finn and ask him to let him pay the mortgage payment next year.

Ralph Finn leaned back in his chair, rubbed his hands together and said, "You got ten days to give me a payment in either gold or silver. Don't care how you get it or what you have to sell, but if you don't pay, I'll own your farm."

It was when Dobi brought his share of the three hundred dollar payment in Memphis bank notes that Eric finally told us what had happened. The bank ate our savings we were going to use to make our mortgage payment. yet we still have to pay back the money we borrowed from the bank. Our only chance was to sell horses, cows, saddles, harness or anything else we could sell. But no one could buy what we had to sell as everyone's money had been lost in the bankruptcy. No one had any gold or silver, which was what Finn demanded. If we took our things to New Orleans to sell we'd not get back in time to make the payment.

I remembered what Crinan had said, "Make them give you gold. If someone tries to give you paper you know someone is trying to cheat someone and you don't want you to be that someone.

The Sheriff and Finn came to our house and told us we had forty-eight hours to evacuate our home. Finn made believe he was compassionate and in a voice dripping in pity said, "you may take those two wagons, the four oxen, the old saddle horse and your clothes. You must leave everything else to pay the balance of your note. That includes all the grain you have harvested. If you take anything else, I'll put you in prison for theft."

CHAPTER V
HOW A PERSON HANDLES ADVERSITY IS A MEASURE OF HIS CHARACTER

ERIC SEEMED TO BE SO CONFUSED that I felt I should speak to Finn about Dobi. I told him Dobi was a freed slave who share cropped the place where he lived and that all the farm implements and tools belonged to him. I suggested that he leave him be as he produced a lot of products for us. Then I rode over to Dobi's house where he was busy packing. I told him what I had told Finn, and that for the present if he were a share cropper it would be better than having no place at all. He agreed and thanked me.

I don't know what we would have done if it had not been for Aunt Ester and the Madison Clan she had married into. Old Man Madison had sold all his slaves. Said they weren't profitable. He had some empty slave shacks and said we could move in there.

There we were that first night, five of us crowded together in a little one-room shack. Eric was like a walking dead person. I put my arm around him and said, "It isn't your fault we lost the farm." You didn't do anything wrong. They got cheap land in Missouri. We can start over. Eric wasn't listening.

He went to the wagon and took a long swig from a jug. When he returned, his face was flushed, and he began talking about crooked lawyers and bankers. After each trip to the wagon his voice got louder. He raved on until dawn, then fell down and went to sleep. I reckoned he had a right to do what he did, considering what happened to us.

It is strange to me why some people's minds get stuck on their losses. In the history father taught us, we learned about whole countries who lost wars, spent money and time thinking about the unfairness of their losses for fifty generations. In the Old Testament almost every chapter tells of the losses about which they mourned for thousands of years. They could have thought about how to get on with what they had left.

Eric went out every day and talked to the people around Memphis. I don't know whether he was trying to get all the hate out or was trying to get people to do something about the banker and Finn. No one paid him any heed because he was always drunk.

We were getting along because our neighbors were very understanding. They were letting the children and me work in exchange for food. And of course, Roy was always plotting ways to make money. My sister Alice helped as much as she could but my mother had lived with her since my father, the minister, died and they too had been hit by the bank failure. Old Finn had bought all the mortgages the bank had for pennies on the dollar before the bank went broke. Most people were allowed to rent the home they had lost, but Finn took a fancy to our place and decided to make it his home and headquarters.

After six months of Eric's drunkenness, Kenneth, Roy, and Rosemary came to me and said they wanted to talk. Kenneth put his arm around me and said, "Papa isn't going to do anything but get drunk. Dobi and Sahara and Martha and Orville have lost their places to Finn, but they are not going around getting drunk. As soon as they can get enough gold to buy more wagons, livestock and provision they plan to load their wagons on a flat boat and go to Liberty Missouri. Then they intend joining a wagon train headed for the Oregon Territory where the land is free for the taking.

"We don't have to go to Oregon." Roy said. "There is cheap land over near Springfield, Missouri. Won't cost us much because we could get their in just a few weeks and be ready to plant next spring."

Kenneth squeezed me again and said, "Roy, Rosemary and me are young and we're going to Missouri. We want you to come with us and leave Papa here."

I was sad that the boys didn't have more understanding of their father but of course they were young. "You're old enough to take care of yourself but I must stay here and take care of papa. How will you get there? You have no money."

"We'll work for hire on the river till we get enough money," Roy said

"As soon as papa gets all the rage out of him we'll go to Missouri," I said.

That night, Eric came home drunk, we thought, but as it turned out he was sick. He was feverish and out of his head. I bathed him in cold water to keep the fever down and gave him sassafras tea. My mama came over every night and prayed for him.

He was sick like that for two weeks, then, he began talking and eating. "When I was sick, the Lord passed into my head and told me I must give up my oldest son and take my family to the promised-land in Missouri," he said.

Kenneth was the tallest Carter that had ever lived and weighed 165 pounds. He was exceptionally strong and had worked for Lawyer Finn training horses on occasions. So, when Eric asked Finn if he would like to indenture Kenneth, he jumped at the chance. Kenneth wasn't all that happy being a sacrificial lamb.

Eric began by telling Kenneth that it was God's Will. That didn't impress Kenneth, who like his grandpa Crinan, thought such things were nonsense. When Eric promised Kenneth that he would own half of the land they would buy in Missouri, Kenneth agreed.

Finn gave Eric five hundred dollars in gold in exchange for a five year indenture contract for Kenneth. I knew it was fair and an opportunity for the whole family, but I was sad. Kenneth was going to be just like a slave and would be a long ways from Missouri.

We visited all our neighbors and spent a week getting ready, and with the help of Martha, Orville and their fifteen-year-old daughter Betsy, we were soon ready to go to Missouri.

Before we lost our home, Betsy had spent a lot of time with us, but the small quarters where we lived now made it difficult for Martha's other two younger children to stay over night with us. So we never got to know them. A boy and a girl, we never got to know and they never got to know us. One of my greatest losses is not getting to know the the younger boy and girl and there not getting to know us.

Orville and Martha sharecropped the place they had once owned but Finn drove such a hard bargain by taking most of what they grew for the rent, this caused them great hardship. As soon as they could save enough to properly provision themselves, they were going to Oregon where there were no banks or lawyers.

Ester held a going away party for us in their barn where all their friends wished us luck and then everyone just waltzed and did the polka all night long. Early the next morning we said good-by to the Tennessee that had been as my father said, "His Promised Land," but Crinan said that for he and Mary it was " The Land of Promise."

As we were preparing to load on the ferry, a flood of Indians from the east began to gather around the ferry. They had been driven from their homes by Jackson's army.

Eric said, they were the Cherokee tribe who had helped his family. He said he must help them. He sent Roy with a note to get Dobi and asked him to come down so they could help the tribe who had helped his family escape Alexander.

Dobi 's arrived within an hour with his whole family in his buggy. Eric asked him why he brought his whole family. Dobi said that he wanted his children to meet some of their relatives. Eric never told me that Dobi was related to these Cherokees. When I asked him why he hadn't told me, he said he had no idea that Dobi was related to this tribe. But he said that Dobi's mother, Sheli, had belonged to the Chief of this tribe during the years that Dobi would have been conceived.

Eric and Dobi worked for a week getting the tribe across the river. Later more Indians appeared and they were followed by a regiment of soldiers. This was too much for Eric and Dobi..

Our two wagons were loaded on the ferry that took us across the Mississippi then we followed a wagon trail west along the north side of the Arkansas River. Eric said it was wilderness like the frontier country where he had traveled forty years ago.

CHAPTER VI
CARTERS MOVE TO MISSOURI

I WAS VERY YOUNG when I came with my parents to Tennessee and didn't remember much about it. But I will never forget the six weeks experience of jarring wagons, sore feet, summer heat, bugs and dust on the way to Springfield, Missouri. Besides all those irritations, Eric was always asking us to pray. He made more fuss about religious etiquette then did my father, a minister.

We stopped for a day in Springfield where we made application to buy land. We looked at the maps and made an agreement to inspect several parcels.

The government had a lot of cheap land for sale near Joplin, Missouri. The rolling hills and wooded creek bottoms would make good pasture, but it wasn't very good for farming. We chose a strip of land that was one half mile wide and two miles long. It was covered with trees except for a flat piece of about 200 acres with a clearing where we could build a house near a creek. Eric returned to Springfield and paid for the land with part of the gold he had received from Finn.

It was early summer, and we had to start plowing and building shelter right away before the fall rains. Eric was no longer young and was often sick. He prayed a lot, but only when someone could hear him. Most of the work was left to Roy and Rosemary. Although Ester sent letters assuring us that Kenneth was doing well, I missed him and looked forward to seeing him.

Martha sent a letter to the store in Joplin every month telling us that they were doing fine and that Orville, her husband, had almost saved enough gold for their trip to the Oregon Territory. She also said that Betsy, who was fifteen, had, become a very good writer and that many of her poems had been published and that she had met a very nice boy but wasn't sure if she wanted to marry just yet.

That first summer Roy chopped down trees in the early morning and then hitched up the oxen and plow until sundown. Rosemary who was just thirteen would trim the branches and bark from the trees and drag them with the oxen to a place near where we were building. The next morning Roy would notch the logs and the two of them with block and tackle would lift them into place on the wall. Then Roy would go back to plowing for the rest of the day while Rosemary drove wooden chinks into any wide places between the logs and sealed everything with a mixture of clay and grass. In this way we built ourselves a very comfortable two-roomed cabin. Eric and I slept in the bunkroom, and Rosemary and Roy each had a bed-roll in the kitchen.

Roy plowed the sod day after day until that one morning in November he brought the oxen back to their shelter. He came into the house and said," Can't plow any more the ground is too frozen."

By spring we had spent most of our money just to survive but the store in Joplin gave us credit and we planted. We had a good crop, but we had no market; consequently money was scarce. It wasn't like Tennessee where we could ship our grain down the river. We were too far from the Arkansas River.

We grew and preserved food from the garden and picked berries from the forest. Although we didn't have any cows or pigs the deer and geese were plentiful.

Roy's mind was always busy thinking about ways of getting cash. He knew prices and when he could buy something that he knew he could sell for more he bought it. When the weather was bad, Roy was often in Joplin just talking to people and dealing. If he couldn't sell tools, furniture or small animals that he had bought to Joplin, he would go to Springfield.

Eric was becoming a problem. His mood was erratic, and he would forget something he had said only five minutes before. Roy and Rosemary stayed away from him as much as they could.

Barely three years had passed of Kenneth's indenture contract, when he rode into our yard on a fine horse and saddle. We all crowded around him with all kinds of questions, but he wouldn't answer any of them. "Wait 'till after supper and I'll tell you everything, he said.

We ate as fast as we could and then waited for his story. This is the story he told:

"Old Finn was a mean spirited, ugly old man and so many people hated him that he had to have a body guard. But I just took all his mean talk and bad treatment 'cause Ester told me you had bought the land and was doing well. I didn't want to cause any trouble and I didn't want to be a hunted man for breaking the indenture contract.

"One night I was in the woodshed where I lived. I heard Finn and his wife yelling' at each other. Then I heard Mrs. Finn scream like she was being hurt and Finn shouted, "I'm going to cut out that bastard child inside you and throw him in the outhouse hole.

"I slipped on my boots, looked out the door into their window and saw him knock her down and started kicking her. She was near the shotgun corner and grabbed the shotgun and pointed it at Finn. I heard it go off.

I went inside to see if I could help. As soon as I got inside the door, she started screaming and hitting at me. I backed out the door just as Tomo, the half-breed bodyguard, came down stairs. I heard Mrs. Finn tell him that I had attacked her and shot Finn. If she were going to tell that lie, no one would believe that I hadn't done what she said. I ran to the stable threw a saddle on the back of the fastest horse, grabbed another expensive saddle and lit out for the ferry. I told the ferry operator that my other horse died and that I didn't need two saddles. He bought the saddle. I used the money to pay for my horse and me to across the Mississippi.

"I know that as long as I am in the states they will be looking for me. So I can't stay here. I've decided to provision up and go to Santa Fe in Mexico."

Eric started raving' again about Jackson and the Democrats. He had made an about face in his political sympathies since the bank had gone bankrupt. He had blamed Jackson for allowing banks to go bankrupt. He said that God would not let him go unpunished. Then he went down on his knees and prayed so loud, it hurt my ears. He didn't pray to help Kenneth, but asked God to take revenge on the Finns.

The rest of the family went to work getting things together for Kenneth. We gave him two pack mules to carry all his provisions and went to Springfield where we bought him a gun and ammunition.

Then we went to the house of a man who drew pictures of the likeness of the whole families. All of our family except Martha and her three children lined up in the man's parlor. He took each of us by our selves and spent thirty minutes drawing our pictures. This will be the first picture of the Carters. Now our descendants will know what we looked like.

I was sad to see Kenneth go, but Rosemary and Roy were excited about the adventures their older brother would have in Santa Fe.

Eric led us in prayer and Kenneth kissed Rosemary and me. As he rode away he shouted back, " I'll get the biggest ranch in Mexico. Then I'll send for you to live in the sunshine year around."

A few years after Kenneth left I heard about people in the West getting filthy rich digging gold right out of the ground. I hoped that Kenneth was one of those who got rich. But we never heard of him again. That has always been a heavy burden on me. I often stay awake all night just wondering about him.

It was in the fall of 1842 when we went to Joplin to get some provisions at the mercantile store where we asked for our post. There were many pages of a letter from Martha and Betsy. We read and re-read all that they had written and delighted in Betsy's talent as a writer especially since she was so young.

As it happened, they were going to join a wagon train in Liberty Missouri and travel to Oregon. Betsy had described Oregon Territory in her fine writing as a paradise with mild winters and cool summers where the plants all grow lush.

Four families would be traveling together. Martha and Orville, Doby and Sahara, the Caldwell Family who were close friends of Martha, and a family who had started from their home in Nashville.

At the time she wrote the letter, they were fixing to put their wagons on a flatboat and travel up the Mississippi to the Missouri, then they would go up the Missouri River to Liberty Missouri, where they would join the big Wagon train in the spring of 1843. They would post another letter when they arrived in Liberty before they joined the big train. We would impatiently wait for the next post.

1843 started out with snow that drifted over the windows on the north and didn't melt until the April rain started. But the rain didn't stop until the middle of May and we didn't get anything planted till June. We'd be lucky if the corn matured.

Closed in for six months with Eric that year was a trial. He was confused all the time and he got so he couldn't remember how to talk, but sometime if you didn't watch out, he would strike out at you.

We finally got a letter from Martha and Betsy in May, though they had sent it in March just before they left. Must have been the weather that caused the delay. They had gotten a place near the front of the Wagon Train that pleased Betsy because she said she would see Charley sooner than if she were at the back of the line of wagons. Betsy said she was thinking about marrying Charlie Meyer when they arrived in Oregon. Charley had gone to Oregon with a pack train in 1842 and had claimed 640 acres of prime land. They could raise a family on that much land.

When we first came to Missouri, we were having trouble selling what we raised and we were always short of cash, but leave it to Roy. He figured out a way to get cash when there was very little of it in the country.

Roy and Rosemary would take a wagon loaded with chickens, geese and pigs or anything else they could think of, tied several horses on the rear and Rosemary herded oxen or cows in front. They traveled along the roads and trails from farm to farm. Some times, they would be out for weeks camping along the way. At each farm, they would try to sell what ever they had for cash but that wasn't often possible since people had so little cash. If a farmer wanted something but couldn't afford to pay cash, Roy would trade for something they had. But he never traded without getting some cash boot.

For instance, if Roy had a horse the farmer wanted and was willing to trade two heifer for the horse, Roy would go on about how good his horse was and degrade the heifers for some time. Then he would condescend to trade but only if they would give him $5.00 cash in addition to the two heifers.

He returned sometimes with the same value in livestock and implements as he started with and have $75.00 cash besides. What is more, he got to see a lot of people that included Lydia who he had asked for her hand in marriage.

Martha had been gone for about a year and a half and I had been expecting a letter for

some time. I was so anxious to hear from them that I often made special trips to Joplin just to ask the post agent if we had any letters.

It was in October of 1845, when I ask him if he had a letter. He said, "No, but I got a sea packet for you. Come by sea to New Orleans from the Oregon Territory." I wanted to open it right off but decided to wait until I could read it to everyone.

That evening when Roy and Rosemary had finished eating and Eric had

Fallen asleep, I announced that we had gotten a letter from Martha and Orville. I opened it up and began reading the many pages. It was a copy of Betsy Roark's Diary that Joan Caldwell had copied.

It said, "I am sending you this, so you will know what happened to the Roarck Family. I have taken the liberty of copying Betsy's Diary as she tells the story much better than I could. I have given the original copy to Betsy's brother and sister.

Betsy began her Diary when she was still in Tennessee at the harvest festival in 1841.

CHAPTER VII

BETSY ROARCK'S DIARY

OCTOBER 15, 1841

We were at the Saturday dance when Charley grabbed my arm and guided me out of a small barn door, past the wagons behind some lilac bushes. He took both my arms and pulled me to him. His fingers bit into my upper arms. I felt a little frightened 'cause he had never been that rough with me before.

He said he needed to talk to me. I ask him why he just didn't come over to our house and talk. I told him it would be fine because papa favors him courting me.

His fingers were hurting my arms. I told him to let go of my arms and speak his mind fast before people got worried about us being behind this bush.

He told me what he had to say was just between him and me and no one's business but ours. He said that since I was going to be his wife, he thought I ought to know what he was fixing to do. I told him to say what he wanted to say so we could go back in before someone missed us

He let go of my arms and said that he knew my family was figuring to go to Oregon in April, and he was going to go with us.

I told him that before we left we could be married, then we could go as a family.

Charley took a deep breath and sighed. He told me that George and Andy was going by packhorse to Oregon next week, and they wanted him to go with them. He said he figured he could get there early and locate the best land for my folks and for us before all the good land got taken up. He also said he would build some shelters for my folks and us cause it would be getting along toward winter when we got there.

I took a deep breath. Charley put up his hand like he was swearing to do something and said, " I swear I'll be careful." He said that Andy had been to Oregon before and went on to say that by the time we got to Fort Laramie they would catch up to some trappers going to Oregon. I hadn't registered any complaint about Charles's plans, but he still went on about what he had heard about how you can get rich selling stuff to California, and how we could have a big house with lots of rooms for lots of children and fine furniture in a parlor with a piano.

Charley always made a lot of sense, which is one of the reasons I liked Charley Meyer. He always told everyone he learned to read and write so he could write the words that said he loved Betsy Roarck. Now he was 18 years old, and said he loves me more than ever. I cannot think of being the wife of any other man. Although he is handsome with blond, wavy hair and powerful muscles, my love is not passionate like I thought it was suppose to be when you marry. He is loyal, honest and very comfortable to be with, like a pair of worn shoes. I may be only fifteen, but I have been alone with many other boys. They are all so shallow and spend all the time trying to impress me with their manliness. It's always a relief to be with Charley.

We went back to the barn where polka music had just ended and the tired dancers left the floor. Raymond Falk, the owner of the Falk Mercantile store, raised his hand and said, "Ladies and Gentlemen, let me have your attention. Colonel Korn has just returned from the Oregon Territory and is willing to share his experience with you tonight. Go ahead Colonel."

The Colonel stood with a bowed head for a moment. Then, as if to reveal a dream, he began a dissertation. He said that in Oregon you can plant corn in April and eat roasting ears in June. The ocean and rivers are full of fish. The winters are warm and the summers are cool. This land with the rich soil is there for the taking. No bankers to foreclose on your farm. No floods, droughts or grasshoppers.

The Colonel went on for an hour until Old Jeb shouted out that Oregon didn't belong to us and asked who was going to protect us from the savages and the British that say they own Oregon.

Raymond Falk waved a piece of paper and with the self-satisfied smile of a cat that just eaten the canary, announced that had a letter dated June 15, 1842 from the Honorable Thomas Hart Benton, the senator from Missouri. He read the letter aloud. It said that after twenty-five years the American population has begun to extend itself to Oregon. Hundreds went a few years ago. A thousand went last year. Two thousand wagons are now setting out from Liberty and Independence Missouri. Tens of thousands are meditating the adventure. Then he raised his hand and read in a loud voice. " I say to you all. Go On! The government will follow you and give you protection."

Then Falk explained that next April, a well organized wagon train would assemble in Liberty, Missouri, and within a fortnight thereafter, leave for Oregon. For many who have suffered the ill effects of Jackson's government who allowed the bankers to fleece its depositors, this would be a chance to recover their losses. He said that if we had the get up- and- go, we should get up and go to Oregon. He announced that tomorrow in the Memphis town square, the organizers of this new expedition would sign us up for the train. Those who wished to put their wagons on the flat boat and travel to Liberty, the riverboat captains would be there to accept our reservations. Falk would be there to take orders for the supplies they would need.

The next day, father and I went to the square to sign up. We saw our neighbors and Dobi who had found working at hard labor for Finn on what was once his own farm to be a hateful existence. He wanted to go to Oregon; however, though the Wagon Expedition would accept his wagon , the flatboat would not haul his wagons because he was a Negro. He would have to cross the Mississippi and travel by land to Liberty through all the winter rain and snow in order to reach Liberty by April. Dobi is old but he seemed to be able to do as much hard work as he ever had. His three sons still have difficulty keeping up with him.

I am the oldest child in the Roarck family and help take care of my brother Jackie, who is eight, and my sister Mary Ann, who is six. Since we lost our farm, both mother and father have been working to get enough money to go to Oregon and I gladly suffered inconveniences for a better future. So when Charley left I didn't complain. After all, he was going to Oregon early for the family we hoped to have some day.

Even though she was four years older than me, Joan Caldwell was my best friend. And on this day in October 1842, when the leaves were turning red the two of us were sitting on the front porch slicing apples for drying and talking up a storm.

I said, "It'll be five months before we get started on our way to the Oregon country. It's such a long time and I am missing Charley real bad." I explained that Charley was going to get 640 acres of fine land for us so we could raise a proper family.

Joan sneered and ask me what makes me think I'll ever see Charlie again?

She doesn't know Charley well enough to know that when he tells me he loves me, he means it.

Then she goes on about him having a silver tongue if he's got me believing him. She said that there wasn't a man alive that would be loyal to a woman if he has to sacrifice what he wants.

I explained to her that Charley and me were not the selfish kind. I said that I know what's good for Charley is good for me and Charley knows what is good for me is good for him. We got an understanding.

Joan was bitter. I could tell when she said, "A man only wants a woman for what she can do for him. Feed him, make his clothes, raise his children and make him feel like a King. Men don't even talk to their women after they marry them except to assign them menial tasks. They got short memories and can't even remember what they said when they were courting."

I asked her why, if she felt that way about men, why would she marry one?

Joan put down her apples and began pacing back and forth on the porch. She was acting like some preacher trying to convince people to be baptized. Three years ago she said Eddie Johnson left her and went to Oregon. He told her he loved her more than life and would be back for her when he got some land in Oregon. She said she hadn't heard a word from him since. She said that if she waited for him, she would be an old maid when he got back. "I am going to marry," she said, " cause you're nobody until you are someone's wife. But I am going to be a rich man's wife because you are more of a somebody if your husband is rich."

I didn't say anything because I was thinking. Oregon is so far away and it will be a whole year before we will be in Oregon. I have a premonition. It is nothing real, just a feeling that makes me sad.

Ezra Ward brought his buggy to a stop a few feet from the porch. He greeted us and asked us if we were going to the October Celebration.

I told him I wasn't going with anyone because I was engaged to Charley and he was in Oregon.

Joan said she wanted go, but there was no one to take her.

Ezra heard that statement and answer immediately. He said, "Joan, I'd be honored to take you to the Celebration, if you'll go with an old man."

Joan said she would go with him if they could go in his surrey with the yellow wheels and the matching bays.

Ezra said he would bring his yellow- wheeled surrey to her house at five and visit with her father and then they would go on to the celebration at six. Then he asked her if that would be all right with her.

She told him she would be waiting.

Ezra slapped the lines on the buggy horse, waved good-by and was soon out of sight.

I ask Joan how she could go with such an old and wrinkled man.

She said that he had 500 head of cattle and lot of money.

I asked her what Eddie would say. She just laughed

JANUARY 30, 1843

I haven't received a letter from Charley. Perhaps he has forgotten me or the letter has gotten lost. Soon we'll be on the flat boat and I won't be able to get a letter from him. I feel so nervous I can't keep my mind on what I am supposed to do. I forgot to milk the cow till after dark.

FEBRUARY 25, 1843

I just got a letter that Charlie wrote last April. He is safe and sound and is enthusiastic about the land he has found for my parents and us. I should feel joy and excitement from his letter, but I still feel forebodings. Father said not to worry for the time will pass, and we'll be in Oregon before we know it.

MARCH 1,1843

Three days later we pulled our wagons on to the flat boat and tied our livestock to posts in the livestock pen. We slowly moved up the Mississippi.

MARCH 30,1843

We have turned up the muddy Missouri that looked like plowed ground. The scenery helps take my mind off how long it will be before we reached Oregon.

APRIL 1,1843

We docked in shallow water and pulled the wagons off the flat boat into water up to the oxen's bellies. No sooner had we gotten our two wagons, the horse and our milk cow off the boat than a man on horseback rode up and yelled instructions. "First in line will be at the head of the train. Good Luck!"

I grabbed father's arm and told him that if we get up in the front, we'll get to Oregon first. Father reckoned that if we got up front we'd have less dirt to eat. But we weren't fast enough. We were about the 10th in line.

APRIL 10,1843

Joan married Ezra last Christmas. and used her feminine- power, as she called it, to convince Ezra to move to Oregon. He was taking twenty wagons, two hundred head of cattle and thirty indentured drivers and herders. Joan and Ezra's two private wagons were in the front and the rest of Ezra's wagons and livestock were in the rear. If Ezra wanted to see how his livestock were doing in the rear, it took all day of hard riding to get to the rear and back to Joan's wagons in front.

We heard that Dobi and family had been the first to be in line but the Wagon Master ordered him to stay at least a mile behind the others. He wouldn't get any cooperative help crossing the rivers like the rest of us, but Dobi didn't care.

THE LAND OF PROMISE

APRIL 15, 1843

Jackie, Mary Ann and I herd our spare oxen and the milk cow behind the wagons while mother and father each walked and drove an oxen team, each pulling a wagon.

APRIL 20, 1843

The tall grass in Kansas-Nebraska country this spring is beautiful. The livestock have plenty to eat and everyone is so optimistic, except me. I am impatient, and every time we cross a river we are slowed down, I am doubly impatient. I feel that we have got to hurry before some misfortune strikes us.

JULY 20, 1843

I am so sad, I haven't been writing much in the Diary, but I have to record what traveling is like now. We have been walking over sand in this God forsaken desert for a month. The July heat and scarcity of grass have weakened the oxen and they move even slower. I don't know how much longer they will last. They say we will reach Fort Laramie in ten days where we will rest and let our animals graze on the tall grass in the North Platte Valley.

JULY 28, 1843

Most every family has at least one gun they had recently bought. They think they will have to fight off the savages. But the Indians are friendly, although they have to be watched after dark, for often they steal livestock. Since few people had a gun back in the states, most of them are still learning to use them. Every evening I hear gunshots fired by people who are learning to use their firearms.

JULY 30, 1843

I knew something would happen. Father was accidentally shot by one of those drifters who was always practicing. I think they just like to hear the noise. We put him in the wagon where mother cleaned the wound in his chest. Mr Harris rode five miles behind us to get a doctor.

JULY 31, 1843

Father woke up a little and mumbled, "All they got in this wagon train are the restless, rootless and fugitives." He went to sleep and never woke again. When the doctor arrived he said father was dead.

AUGUST 1,1846

Mother did not cry. I don't know why. Jackie and Mary Ann sobbed all night long. Some men dug a four- foot deep grave and the next morning at sunrise, Preacher Jonah said some words I couldn't understand as they lowered father into his grave. Before the grave was filled in, wagons started moving. I heard someone say, "The grave is so shallow, wolves will dig him up and chew his bones.

AUGUST 3,1843

Though I am small, I can still drive oxen. So I drive the ox team behind mother while Jackie and Mary Ann herd the rest of the livestock. Everyone says we should stay in Fort Laramie and go back to the states with someone who will be going east. I've got to argue mother to keep on going. I'll tell her that Charlie will take care of her and the kids. Even though she can't own land, we can put the land in Jackie's name, because he is a boy and when he is eighteen he'll have 640 acres. If she doesn't go on, I'll go on with Joan.

AUGUST 4,1843

I didn't need to worry as Mother was not in an arguing mood when she raised her voice to those who wanted her to go back. She said she didn't start this trip with the idea of going back, if things didn't go just right. She told them that she was responsible for raising her and Orville's children and she didn't want to raise them back there where all the politicians and bankers tell people what to do. "Besides", she said, "we need a clean land where people don't get the fever all the time."

SEPTEMBER 15, 1843

We have just left this crazy river that winds like a snake across the land and almost every day we have another river crossing. They say we're already in Oregon territory. But I am feeling awful puny. I can hardly walk. Mother is trying to find someone to take my wagon until I get feeling better. The doctor says I have the fever.

SEPTEMBER 18,1843

The rules of the wagon train are that a person who has the fever must stop and let the rest of the train pass and then follow a mile behind. I can't write any more so mother has promised to keep up my diary.

SEPTEMBER 30,1843, (Written by Martha.)

I have promised Betsy to keep up her diary

I have made a soft bed for Betsy in my wagon and left one wagon behind. She is so tiny, not even five feet tall. As she sleeps, I look at the sweat soaked blond hair sticking to her pretty oval face and ask myself. Why had God done this to her? Why Betsy, who is so smart and full of life and promise when he lets the likes of that trash who shot Orville live on?

OCTOBER 5,1843

As we start into the Blue Mountains Jackie and Mary Ann are herding the cow and the oxen a good distance ahead of the wagon. I see snow on the peaks. I hope we don't get any snow. The train is moving faster now. We can hardly keep up. I guess they want to get through the mountains before winter storms come.

OCTOBER 10,1843

I must have been careless. A front wheel dropped into a hole and when I struck the oxen to make them pull hard, the wheel broke. Turbulent clouds are coming in, and we will perish if we stay here. I have loaded what I can on the oxen and tied Betsy on Old Joe, the strongest ox.

OCTOBER 12, 1843

We are keeping up now but Betsy moans and cries all the time. It is breaking my heart, but I don't know what else to do. Betsy is begging me to let her off the ox so she can die. I thought she was out of her head. I took her off and laid her on a quilt. She is begging me in a whisper not to put her back on the ox. "Let me die," She mumbles. She insists that I promise her to bury her deeper than they did her father. She is afraid the wolves will dig her up. I took her in my arms and promised her. She seemed to be relieved.

OCTOBER 13, 1843

Jackie road our saddle horse in a full out gallop to get someone in the train to help dig Betsy's grave. The first person he saw was Dobi and his oldest son riding mules. They had heard of our misfortunes and were the only ones strong enough to brave the possibility of getting the fever.

After they had dug about four feet they got out of the hole. Betsy was lying near by and when they quit digging I heard Betsy breath heavily like she was trying to say something. I jumped into the hole and began digging. I said that I promised Betsy we would dig six feet into the ground. Dobi jumped into the hole and at eighty-seven years old dug it to about seven foot deep.

Betsy asked to be placed over near her grave so she could look into it. The sun was getting low, so we built a fire to keep Betsy warm. She whispered weakly and I put my ear near her mouth so I could hear her. She said, " Please tell Charley that I love him and that I am so sorry I died." I promised. She seemed to relax, closed her eyes and in about thirty minutes she stopped breathing. Dobi felt for a heart beat and shook his head and looked into some bushes as if he had lost something.

After we filled in the grave, Abraham, Dobi's Son, brought Jackie and Mary Ann and the livestock in. We built a wall from the flat stones near by as a marker. I said I would come back later and put a proper stone there.

OCTOBER 15, 1843

Joan heard about our trouble and sent several men back to help us. But it was too late. They told me they would herd our livestock with theirs and one of the men in a buggy took the kids and me to the front of the train where I rode with Joan in her wagon.

OCTOBER 30, 1843

I am so thankful for Joan. I don't feel too well now. Joan has made me a bed in the wagon. Since I am too weak to write, I asked her to write about things in Betsy's Diary that I had promised to keep up.

(This is Joan Ward writing} I have promised to keep up Betsy's Diary as her mother is too sick to keep it up like she promised Betsy.

NOVEMBER 5,1843

Mrs. Roarck is so sick we can't go on.. The doctor from Fort Dalles says she has Pneumonia.

NOVEMBER 10,1843

This morning the doctor said Mrs. Roarck is dead.

NOVEMBER 12,1843

Charley arrived today as he heard that the wagon train would arrive at Fort Dalles. After hearing of the tragedy that happened to the Roarck family, he insisted that he would take Jackie and Mary Ann and give them a good home. Many in the train are appalled at the idea of a man raising two young children where one was a girl. Of all people, quiet, gentle Charley raised his voice to those people he called hypocrites. He said those with the dirty minds who envisioned sexual sins have committed the much greater sin of omission by failing to help the Roarck family. He took the children with him to Oregon City where the brothers and sisters of his beloved Betsy will probably have everything they need to become good people.

JUNE 5 1844

The people of Oregon City, although they do not own slaves, demanded that Dobi leave the territory. He has taken his family across the Columbia River to Fort Vancouver that is owned by the British, who accepts Negroes as citizens. I haven't heard of them for a long while.

Ezra died about three months after we arrived in Oregon, and I married Eddie Johnson.

I located Charley and expect to meet him at the river crossing today where I will give Betsy's Diary to Jackie. I hope you receive this copy I made of Betsy's Diary.

As I read the Diary, I had to stop from time to time to catch my breath. Rosemary held her head in her arms and sobbed. Roy went to look out the window.

After I finished reading, I couldn't control myself and had to go into my bedroom and cry myself into exhaustion. Eric could understand that something had upset me but he could not understand what had happened to Martha and what was causing me to cry.

For six months after I read Betsy's diary I didn't feel like doing anything. It seemed that I had lost everything. I didn't feel like writing and only did it if Roy or Rosemary urged me. Papa was no longer a person and he often struck out at me. Either Rosemary or Roy always had to be around to protect me from Eric. This interfered with their trading trips, and made me feel bad.

We read the Springfield newspaper as often as we could get one and knew that the country called Texas was fighting with a country called Mexico. It also said that Texas wanted to become part of the United States. From what I had heard of Texans I would prefer Mexico keep them..

Then some time later I read that the United States was at war with Mexico. I didn't have much time to think about such things as a bunch of young men taking pot shots at each other. It wasn't any of my business anyway until a couple of the county officials came to our house one evening. They said that General Winfield Scott had asked for more soldiers for his Army. I guess Missouri agreed to send some men. They said that they wanted young single men that owed it to their country to help defeat Mexico

Roy arrived a short time later and was informed of their official mission and why he should become a soldier. Roy walked up to the speaker as if he were going to slap him down, stared fiercely. I heard his words explode, "You tell that Polk and those crooked Democrats that I don't owe them a dammed thing. They owe me, and my family and many honest people millions of dollars. Let me tell you what your government has done to many honest hard working people. First, they sold the land we had cleared, farmed and built our houses on to bankers for the price of a run downed spavined horse, without so much as a "how do you do" to us. Of course the bankers were happy to sell us our property for ten times more than they paid for it. Then when the bankers and their political friends became rich on other people's money, they closed the banks and absconded with the people's savings.

134

"You are part of that government and I smell you and its making me sick. I suggest you get off my property before I really get mad."

The Officials mounted their horses, and as they left, one of them said, "We will remember you and don't you forget it."

When Roy came in, I walked over to him, put my arm around his neck and told him that he shouldn't make enemies of those people for they could do him harm. I didn't want to lose any more of my children.

He told me that if they thought this war created by arms merchants and their political allies was so important, why didn't they and their children join their puppet generals and risk their own lives.

I AM ROSEMARY AND I WISH TO ADD TO WHAT MAMMA HAS WRITTEN IN THE CARTER STORY.

The next morning after Roy had refused official recruitment efforts I went to awaken mamma and found her with her eyes open staring at the ceiling. When I told Roy about mamma he came to verify what I had told him, he noticed that Papa had not moved. He went to see how he was and found him dead.